Scribe Publications
MEASURING UP

G. J. (Gabrielle) Stroud is a primary
school teacher who loves reading and
writing fiction. *Measuring Up* is her
first YA novel. Gabbie lives by the sea
with her baby, Olivia, her husband,
Matthew, and her loyal dog, Shirley.

*Thanks Bob &
Theresa —
you encouraged
me every step
of the way. ♡ Gab ⊗*

MEASURING UP

G. J. STROUD

G Stroud

SCRIBE
Melbourne

Scribe Publications Pty Ltd
PO Box 523
Carlton North, Victoria, Australia, 3054
Email: info@scribepub.com.au

First published by Scribe 2009

Text design by Henry Rosenbloom
Printed and bound in Australia by Griffin Press
Only wood grown from sustainable regrowth forests is used
in the manufacture of paper found in this book

National Library of Australia
Catalogue-in-Publication data

Stroud, G. J., 1977-

Measuring up

9781921372902 (pbk.)

A823.4

www.scribepublications.com.au

For Jess

Dan was always first in and last out. Run and dive, like he was in command. No mighty ocean would ever stand in his way. He seemed to have the surf sussed. We wondered if he had balls of steel.

Ferret followed Dan. Full of bravado, then dumped by the very first wave. He could never time it right. He'd go down like a sack of shit and come up choking. You almost felt sorry for him. Almost.

Mel hardly ever swam. She loved the beach but hated bikinis. If she did go in, she moved slowly, savouring the moment. Or delaying the pain.

And me? I went with respect.

The ocean's a lot bigger than I am.

1

My brother calls me Feet, short for foetus. He was five when Mum was pregnant with me. And curious. Lincoln wanted to know all the details so Mum explained that I was still growing. She told him I wasn't a baby yet, just a foetus. Link loved the word.

'Mum's having a foetus.' He told everyone. Apparently, he could quote the due date and explain the concept of trimesters. And the worst part was that I was trapped, floating around in embryonic fluid. I couldn't even tell him to shut up.

Link's still a freak. Twenty-two and doing Arts at Canberra Uni. He's already got his Masters in BS. He bullshits his way through everything. People don't seem to notice him crapping on; he's like a celebrity.

He's not that bad — only brother I've got. I just wish he'd call me Jonah. Not Feet. I'm not some unformed little sprog anymore. But there's no point arguing. Link's response is always the same: 'You don't get it, do ya, Feet? You're nothing yet. Your life hasn't even started.'

Like I said — he's full of crap.

Just after Christmas, Mum and Dad were off to

the Whitsundays. Mum said she needed 'real sun', as though ours in Merimbula was a cheap imitation. She didn't trust me to be home alone and insisted that I go to Canberra and stay with Link. That annoyed me because Link could've come home and stayed with me. He usually does — bums the whole summer break at Mum and Dad's calling *me* a foetus. If I'm a foetus, he's a sponge. But not this summer. He came down for Christmas Day and that was it.

'Can't you just stay here?' We were struggling up the rocks from Short Point Beach. It was Christmas morning and the surf had been good. I thought he might change his mind. 'It's five weeks, Link. Look what we'll be missing.'

We turned to stare at the surf below. Perfect sets were rolling in and the water was clear. We watched a young kid catch a neat little wave and ride it all the way in.

'I can't. Not right now.' Link shook his head like a wet dog, letting droplets spill over me.

'What's the problem? Uni doesn't start till February and I'm about to do Year 12. I just want to start the year right, you know?'

'I'm not staying, so shut up.' He slapped me on the back, his palm burning into my skin.

I headed for home without him, but Link didn't seem to care.

Halfway down our street I met Dad staggering up the hill with his ancient longboard. I was surprised to see him. He hardly ever surfed — he said it wasn't a suitable pastime for the local senior sergeant.

'What're you doing, mate?' He put his board down and wiped the sweat from his face. 'I thought you and Link were surfing.'

'We were. Link's still there.' The asphalt was boiling under my feet.

'Come and have a hit with your old man,' Dad said, reclaiming his board and gesturing for me to turn around.

I stepped onto the grass and thought about going back for a surf with Dad. Then I remembered Link and that stinging slap on the back.

'Maybe later.' I trudged down the hill to our house and dumped my gear in the garage. Then I sat out on the deck and waited for them to come home. I told myself I wasn't sulking.

They finally wandered back down the hill. Link was talking nonstop, probably dribbling some crap about uni. Dad had his head down. They paused outside our front yard and I watched them rest their boards against the fence. Link was still talking.

Dad stretched out his quads, leaning his weight against the fence. I wondered if he'd be able to walk the next day. Mum'd spew if he did an injury before the big trip.

Link suddenly looked up at me on the deck, as though he'd known I was there all along.

'Hey, Feet!' he called out. 'Get us a beer, would ya?'

'Get it yourself.'

Five weeks in Canberra with Link. I couldn't wait.

Boxing Day was stinking hot and the last place I wanted to be was stuck in a car with my brother heading towards our nation's capital. The salty coolness of my morning surf had quickly evaporated and by the time we reached the city I was already counting the days until I'd be home.

Link had a flat in Watson, a northern suburb of Canberra. The place was dingy with mismatched furniture and curtains that were always closed. Used plates and cups were left to rot like skanky ornaments.

Link directed me to the lounge room. He dumped my bag on an extended sofa bed that looked suspiciously slept in.

'You can sleep here.'

I pulled at the sheet and it lifted up in one stiff, wrinkled piece.

'Nice,' I said, raising my eyebrows.

'Mum doesn't work here.' Link poked me in the chest and sauntered through to the kitchen.

A large poster of Pamela Anderson in all her red-swimsuit glory beamed down from the wall. I loved her in those *Baywatch* pictures, before she got her tits pumped up to the max. She looked more real back then, like she might even go for a guy like me. I smiled up at her.

On the opposite wall, twice the size of Pam, was

another poster. It featured a naked man, done in black and white. He had dark skin and he was *big*. Too big for Speedos, this guy would probably even bust out of boardies. It was meant to look arty — sexy and erotic — but there was something not quite right. And I don't just mean his dick. The look in his eyes, like he was starving. I wondered if Pam might need her heavy-duty tits after all.

I straightened the crusty sheets and tried not to look at the black dude. Instead, I thought of the beautiful surf I was missing. It was early afternoon and the sand bar off Main Beach would be pumping. I could imagine Dan soaking it up. Ferret would be causing havoc out the back, cutting people off on his little boogie board. If the day was nice, Mel might even be there watching them.

I was almost homesick but then Link's flatmate strolled past. Katerina was older than Link, another Arts student. She was peeling off her top as she walked and I caught a glimpse of her smooth, tanned stomach. I looked at Pammy and back at Kat. A few weeks here mightn't be so bad.

But then Link came in, beer in hand and shirt off. He scratched his belly and sat down. There was a moment of silence. Then he stood up and farted in my face.

Living with Link was like being on a whole different planet. No one got out of bed before ten. People came and went. Drugs were smoked and swallowed and sniffed. Sex was joked about and alcohol flowed like tap water. I tried to imagine myself living this exact life twelve months from now, but the stress of the HSC consumed me. I couldn't imagine the day after the exams, let alone the year.

Link was more focused than the others. He had a basic routine: a late sleep-in to recover from the night before, then gym, followed by hours in the bathroom. Most afternoons he went out. He never said where he went and I was never invited. Nights were always the same. Link cooked for the odd selection of people that had accumulated in the flat. If Link felt like going out, they'd all go. If not, they'd stay in. He was the alpha-male that Mel would laugh about. Everyone would be talking and joking, but always looking towards him.

None of that surprised me. Link was a natural. A natural person. People were his thing. Part of me admired that, but what was he really doing? Cooking dinner, crapping on and smoking pot.

The gym was new though and I was surprised to see how strong he was. He worked out for at least two hours every day. He had his own weights set up in the garage. I'd never thought of Link as being strong, having muscles. Surfing was our sport. We didn't do anything else — not seriously.

'Why do you do this?' I was spotting him as he bench-pressed a big bar of weights.

'Fourteen, fifteen.' He exhaled and dropped the bar back onto its cradle. 'I dunno.' He rubbed a towel over his face and shoulders. 'Kat's brother sold me the gym stuff and since there's no surf here, I just started doing it.' He wandered over to the tiny mirror he had propped in the corner. 'And now I look magnificent.' He flexed.

'You do.' I admitted. 'You look good. Even better than when you were surfing.'

Link kept posing and I took in his solid quads and the hard straight lines of his back. His chest and abs were firm and there was more bulk around his shoulders and neck. He thumped his chest like Tarzan.

'You should try it.' He gestured to the bench and I shrugged, taking his place under the bar. He explained the best posture and technique.

'This'll be good for you, Jonah.'

My name. It was nice to hear it.

I liked working out with Link. We started a routine of long runs in the morning washed down with fortified protein shakes. Link had me taking a heap of different muscle-boosting vitamins and he worked me like a dog. He was a relentless trainer and genuine praise was hard to earn.

Flirting was another uni pastime I decided to try. On New Year's Eve I tried to hit on Katerina. Link had a party in his flat: millions of people wall-to-wall. I'd had a lot to drink and so had she. We were sweating it out in the kitchen on the unofficial dance floor. The music was crap — straight from Link's collection. Madonna was begging us to strike a pose and Kat was using me as a prop, posing and pouting around me while I tried to anticipate her moves. I reached for her hand and gave it a kiss, trying to draw her towards me. Even pissed as a newt she'd laughed and slapped me away. Told me I was just a baby and not to waste my time on her.

I didn't kid myself, I knew I had no chance with Katerina, but we had a lot of fun together. Since my bed was in the lounge room, she would often hop in with me. We'd lie there and watch TV or use the PlayStation. It wasn't anything hot, more like she was cuddling in with the family pet.

I was out of control whenever Kat was near me. The first time she crawled in with me, Ferret's voice had sprung into my head like the voice of Satan. *She's a hottie. You should bang her.* Kat was leagues beyond me though and even I knew you didn't 'bang' a beautiful woman. You were meant to make love to them and apparently that was something very different to having a root.

She just wanted to talk anyway. And it's a good thing she was happy to fill in the silence. I loved having her beside me but I had no idea what to say.

I was sure she'd sense my virginity and expose me for the inexperienced kid that I was. She didn't though, she just stared up at the black dude while I gazed at Pam.

Most of the time, I was trying to hide my erection while following the drift of the conversation. Kat never seemed to notice my hard-on and sometimes she'd lie on her side with her tits falling everywhere beneath her t-shirt. I'd stare at Pamela Anderson, amazed that this was my safest option.

After a while I'd calm down and the blood would start circulating back to my brain. Then I'd try to talk. It was like she really wanted to hear what I was saying.

'I wish I could meet a guy like that.' Kat looked up at the Mr Big poster and playfully kicked her leg at him.

'Really?' My little pecker shrunk away.

'Yeah.' She sighed.

''Cause he's got a massive dick?'

'No.' Kat sat up and looked at me. 'Because he's self-assured. Look at him. He knows what he wants. He's determined and decisive. He doesn't want to be friends. He wants action.'

'That's 'cause he's got a big dick.'

Kat laughed and flicked her hair round. 'Yeah. Probably. I mean a big dick's a good thing! But you could have an industrial-sized hose down there and it means nothing if you don't know what you want.'

'Yeah?' The industrial-sized hose momentarily distracted me.

'Yeah.' She turned on her side and her breasts followed, one of them gently grazing against me. I felt my dick firming up. 'So are you going to follow in your brother's footsteps?'

'Sorry?' By now I was out of control and hoping

my penis would grow to industrial proportions.

'You know — his big break; the new job.' She wriggled her fingers in the air to put the words *new job* in inverted commas. I looked at her and tried to think about what she was saying. Suddenly, her phone rang, vibrating between us and sending me crazy as she fumbled around to answer it. Her tits were on the loose and the blood continued pounding in my groin. She rolled off the bed and wandered away talking animatedly. At the doorway she blew me a kiss.

'Beat that,' I said to the black dude.

'Where do you go?' I asked Link the next day. We were wiping down equipment slick with sweat.

'Go?'

'Yeah. You know. Most arvos when you nick off after weights.'

Link paused, towel resting on a worn and cracked training bench. 'Shops.'

'Liar.' I flicked him with the towel and he flicked me back; double strength. 'Just friggin' tell me,' I said, rubbing the welt on my ribs.

He sat down and plucked at the foam bulging from the cracked bench.

'You can't tell Mum.'

I nodded.

'Or Dad.'

I nodded again.

'You can't tell anyone.'

'Yeah, righto. What is it? You've joined the secret service?'

'I've dropped out of uni.'

'Really?' I sat down on the other end of the bench and tossed my towel on the floor. 'Mum'll freak! She'll go ballistic.'

'She won't know,' Link insisted.

'Hey, I'm not going to tell her, but she'll find out, won't she? I mean, sooner or later, you'll have to tell her.' I paused, imagining Mum hearing the news. Then I laughed. 'She's gonna kill you.'

'Shut up.'

I stopped joking and looked at him.

'I've got a job. The pay's good and it's going to get better. I'm building a career and once I've got something to show for it, I'll tell Mum.'

'So what is it?' I looked at him with a million crazy thoughts running through my mind. Pro weightlifter. Bouncer. Drug dealer.

'Modelling.'

I stared at him, trying to work out if he was for real.

'I'm modelling. It's just a few small things right now, but my agency says I've got potential and I've already made some good money. I'm covering the rent, so that's okay.'

He looked at me with a face I'd never seen before. I didn't know what to say.

'And I'm good at it, Joe. I really like it and the shots look great. Different, hey? Like you don't even recognise yourself sometimes, but they're good and I'm meeting heaps of awesome people.'

That same face again. And I realised, for the first time ever, my big brother wanted my approval.

'Good for you, Lincoln.' I held his gaze. 'Good for you.'

'Thanks,' he said smiling. 'You can clean the rest of this.'

He kicked the towel at my feet and walked out of the shed.

That night I dreamt I was having sex, except instead of a penis I had an enormous industrial-sized hose. Women were queuing up for me to service them and next in line was Pamela Anderson, only when she came closer she morphed into Mum and started screaming at me for letting Link quit uni. I woke up feeling horrified and exhausted, trying to tally up how many joints I had shared the night before.

There wasn't a clean glass in the kitchen. Two strangers were asleep at the table. Uni living was starting to get to me. I acted like I didn't care, but I just wanted a clean bed and a toilet without permanent skid marks. I missed the surf and the sea breeze.

Year 12 loomed ahead of me like a massive grey fog. I couldn't imagine getting through it to enjoy a life of hung-over haphazardness like Link did. I wanted order and calm — some sign that life could be controlled and navigated. I needed Mel.

The next day I bummed money from Link, put credit on my phone and called her.

'How're your holidays?' I pulled at the hairs on my leg.

'Yeah, okay. Yours?'

'Alright. I'm over it though. Living here is like being on a never-ending school camp. I can't study.'

'Don't stress. You'll be back in routine soon and you can catch up.'

'Mmm. I hope.' I scribbled little crosses on an old pizza box.

'Dan and Stacey are back together. They broke up for about four hours over New Year's.'

I was keen to know if Mel had hooked up with anyone for New Year's, but she didn't say. And I wasn't going to ask. I remembered my dismal effort with Kat and was glad that none of my mates had been there to see me.

I listened as Mel crapped on about our friends from school. It was chick-shit and I knew it. Guys can smell it a mile away. I was usually immune to the stuff. Girly gossip and bitchy backstabbing didn't interest me. But I just wanted to touch base with home, to remember my real life. Mel kept telling me I wasn't missing anything and to live it up while I could.

'And get this,' she said, giggling. 'Ferret got into a wave-rage fight. Some guy from Melbourne cut him off and you know how Ferret always wears his snorkel mask? He followed the guy to the car park with his mask and flippers still on. The guy from Melbourne goes, "I'm about ready to punch you, mate, but I wouldn't like to hit a guy with glasses."'

I laughed. The world was good again.

'And Jonah?' Mel paused.

'Yeah.'

'There's something I have to tell you, but not on the phone.' Her voice was frail but I didn't fall for it. I'd had enough chick-shit for one night.

'Okay. I'm home on the twentieth. Tell me then.'

Talking with Mel had been a good thing. I stopped stressing about what I was missing and started enjoying what I was doing. Between the morning runs and the afternoon weights, I managed to do some study. It felt a bit like boot camp and I was surprised how much I liked it.

There was no pleasing Link though. Some days it seemed like everything about me annoyed him.

'What are you wearing?' He looked disgusted.

'Clothes?' I wondered if it was a trick question.

Link shook his head. He had just run me through a gruelling track on the back of Mount Majura. Now I was devouring my reward: a thick, chalky protein shake and a big feed of eggs on toast. Link had just finished his beauty routine.

'I'm taking you shopping,' he said.

'Why?' I groaned, looking down at my clothes and trying to see what he saw. I was wearing my school sport shorts and a stripy t-shirt that I'd had since Year 9. Link was dressed like some kind of Mafia boss in blue jeans and a black muscle t-shirt. His dark hair was gelled into style and, despite the heat, he was wearing leather shoes.

'Anyway,' I said, chasing a last bite of egg from my plate, 'I don't have any money for clothes.'

'My shout. Hurry up.' Link jangled his keys and stuffed his wallet into his back pocket.

The Belconnen Mall was throbbing with loud music broken only by screaming toddlers and frustrated parents. Bored Canberra kids roamed the place like it was their second home. I thought of the beach and counted the days until I could be there.

Link dragged me through the shops. I tried on shorts and cargo pants, collared shirts and jackets. He was relentless and seemed to have some vision of what he wanted to achieve. I felt like an idiot every time I stepped out of the change room.

'God, Feet — at least try.' He adjusted my clothes with a skill I thought only mothers possessed. 'You don't want to look like an eight-year-old all your life.'

'Get stuffed.' I stepped into the change room and slammed the door. Link was putting everything on his credit card. I tried to feel grateful.

'Okay — now some shoes.'

'Nah, Link. I'm over it. I don't need shoes down the coast anyway.'

He shook his head. Rolled his eyes. Looked like Mum.

'What?' I opened my hands. 'I don't care about clothes. Just because you're some kind of poofter model now doesn't mean I am too.'

'Hey.' Link turned, pushing me in the chest. 'Don't say that.'

'What? Poofter? I didn't mean *you* were a poofter. You're just acting like one.'

'Shut up.'

'Why?'

'It's not cool, alright? Being gay is just being gay. I don't want to hear you saying that other stuff.'

'Who are you? Dad?'

Link sighed and backed off. 'It's not cool, okay? Poofter's not PC.'

'PC?'

'Politically correct. It's offensive.'

I looked at my brother with new eyes.

'Are you gay?'

He didn't answer straight away. Around us, the mall throbbed and hummed like a living being.

'No, Feet. I'm not gay.'

'Okay.'

'Okay.'

He put me in a headlock and dragged me off to buy shoes.

That night Mel rang me.

'Do you know what PC means?' I said.

'Politically correct. Where'd you hear a big acronym like that?'

'Very funny. I'm serious. You should see Link these days. He's a freak. He's all PC about homos.'

'Homosexuals?'

'Yeah. We had a fight about it because I said *poofter*.'

'Well, it's not a nice word. Everyone has their own sexual compass and we shouldn't judge others by their —'

'Alright, don't start.'

'I won't. So tell me again, when are you getting back?'

'Day after tomorrow. What'd you do today?'

'Hung out with Ferret.'

A rip of jealousy flashed through me. 'But you hate Ferret.'

'Hate's a strong word.' Mel's as PC as they come. 'Plus I needed someone to talk to.'

'So you talked to Ferret?'

'No — I hung out with him. Then I remembered that you can never really talk to Ferret and decided to call you, which is what I'm doing right now.'

'Okay, so what do you want to talk about?'

'Nothing,' she said. 'I'll see you on Saturday.' She hung up on me but I kept the phone to my ear. That's how it was with Mel sometimes. I just couldn't get enough.

The next day Link came into the lounge room with his chest puffed out like he'd just won the Rip Curl Pro.

'Check it out,' he said, flicking off the TV. He dropped a pile of junk mail on my lap.

'What?'

'Just check it out.' He was psyched. I leafed through the catalogues, each one screaming at me about amazing savings and super sales.

'And you're showing me these because ...' I let my voice trail off as Link rummaged among the pile.

'Here, this one.' He shoved it into my hands and I looked through each page.

I nodded. 'Twenty per cent off is a good deal, but I thought we bought all my clothes the other day.'

'Page nine.' He leant over me and flipped the flimsy sheets impatiently.

'Catalogues have page numbers?'

'There.' He jabbed his finger at a page advertising jocks. A man's torso modelled the undies in four different colours.

'And?' I shrugged.

He pointed again. 'That's me. My body. I'm the model.'

I looked again at the torso. The head was not shown and only parts of the legs were visible.

'Link, it's a K-Mart catalogue.'

'So?'

'So I can't even see your head.'

'Well I know it's me.'

'Yeah, I know it's you,' I lied. 'But like, you've done other stuff, right? This isn't the only job. I mean you're not going to rock up to Mum with these headless jock shots and expect her to —'

'I'm *so* glad I showed you.' His sarcasm filled the room.

I inhaled a deep breath of it and tried to say the right thing. 'It's a good start though. If modelling's what you want to do.'

'You reckon?' He looked at me like I usually looked at him.

'For sure,' I picked up the catalogue and studied the photos again. 'I mean of course they can't use your face because you're so butt ugly.'

'You peckerhead.' He snatched the catalogue from me and studied the shots. 'You know they asked me if I had a little brother but I told them our mother ate you at birth.'

I laughed. 'And you're next. She'll eat you alive when she finds out you left uni.'

Link looked at me and smiled. 'You gotta die somehow.'

2

'What have you done to my boy?' Mum glared at Link before crushing me in a hug. 'And where did you get these clothes?'

'Do you like them?' I still felt like I was wearing a costume.

'You look fine, mate.' Dad offered me a handshake and pulled me in for a hug.

'You look good too, Mum.' Link was quick. 'Look at that tan.' He let out a slow wolf-whistle that had Mum grinning and forgiving him all at once.

'Well, come on you lot, we can't stay long.' Our dad, Senior Sergeant Worthy, was always the picture of efficiency after a holiday. Link carried my stuff down to the car and I trailed after him with a large garbage bag.

Dad struggled as he tried to jam the boot closed. 'What is this?'

'Some of my old stuff for Feet.' Link pushed at the bag, morphing it into a flatter shape.

'Well I hope you've left yourself something to wear.' Mum pushed against the boot and I thought of the tangled mess of clothes spewing from Link's wardrobe.

'It's Feet you need to worry about, Mum. He came here looking like an orphan.'

'Feet looks fine.' Mum clucked her tongue in frustration. 'We've got to stop calling him that.' She hugged Link ferociously, kissing him twice on both cheeks. 'Double love, Handsome.'

The road from Canberra to Cooma is a boring, predictable highway and the one to Nimmitabel isn't much better. Faded paddocks stretch endlessly on either side with lonely sheep and rugged trees occasionally breaking the view. But once you're over Brown Mountain, it's like the world opens up. The paddocks become green again and the hills stand together forming valleys. Even the roads become exciting, finding their way between peaks to reveal little scenes that look like they should be in picture frames.

The last five kilometres bringing you into Merimbula are the best. The road creeps and twists upward through thick, dry bush. You can't see what's ahead until the road stops climbing and straightens out. Then suddenly the bush steps back, like curtains opening on a stage. Revealed in sheer abundance is the ocean. That view from the hill means just one thing: I'm home.

Dad drove into town doing about forty and noting every change. I wanted to get out and make a run for it, straight to the surf. When he turned into Lakeview Avenue, I got a smooth feeling of calm.

Finally, I could breathe again.

Mum and Dad were still emerging from the garage as I tucked my board under an arm and headed down the driveway.

'Jonah?'

I groaned. 'What?'

'Have a good time.' Mum shook her head and smiled.

'Love ya!' I jogged out the driveway and up the hill.

Mel lived two doors up and the rule was that if I was surfing at Bar I had to invite her. Bar Beach was the perfect spot for families with young kids. There were no waves and if you timed it right, you could catch an awesome current as the lake drained into the sea. But, about fifty metres out, off the bathwater beach was a sand bar that kicked up some of the nicest waves known. Mel loved the calm and I loved the wild — Bar was the best of both.

'Holy shit!' Mel said as she stepped out onto her veranda. 'Look at you.'

'What?' I couldn't stand another bagging about the stupid new clothes.

'You look like a grown-up.' Mel giggled. 'It's like you've got your first bra and your periods all on the same day. Tell me — have you shaved your legs?'

'Get stuffed,' I mumbled, dumping my board and leaning against the decking.

Mel laughed. 'You've even got PMS.'

I belted her on the arm and on reflex, she slapped me.

'I missed you.' She turned back into the house.

'Me too.'

We walked up the hill and then back down the side road. Mel led the way through the Rotary Tourist Walk, taking two shortcuts that took us down onto Bar. On the sand, Mel went to our usual spot and started unpacking her enormous beach bag as though she was moving in for a week. I stripped off what I had come to think of as my Canberra Clothes and stumbled into the boardies Mel handed me.

'It's a sad reflection on our relationship that you can just stand in front of me in your jocks.'

'You should try it.' I winked at her and she poked out her tongue.

The water was cool as it licked over my skin. I paddled out to the bar and nosed a place among the other surfers. It was late afternoon and pretty quiet; most of the punters were safe in their overpriced accommodation preparing for a night on the town. I spotted a few lads I knew and gave them a nod.

I was noodle-armed and weak as I fought to catch my first wave. The recent weeks of bicep curls and bench presses weren't the same as a strong paddle stroke and I cursed Link for making me stay away. The wave was solid and I caught it easily, pumping for speed. As the swell subsided, I slipped down on my board and paddled back out. Resting on the gentle back waters, I sat up on my board and grinned, letting the endorphins rush through me. It was good to be home.

The waves were steady and consistent with no hint of wind. I'd caught a heap of good rides and was just starting to feel tired when the mother lode arrived. It was one big set — the kind that Ferret called tsunamis. The first few waves were full and watery, too round and swollen to catch. But the last ones were perfect. Sharp and intense, just begging to be picked up and brought home. I let the other fellas go first and waited till the set had nearly finished. I swam hard to get on and she delivered. I slid across the face, clean and smooth. I could feel the air drying my skin and the pressure of the wave moving beneath me. I was suspended in time and nothing else mattered. It was like I was vacuum-packed — just me and the wave.

I let my shadow fall across Mel's sun, the way I knew she hated.

'Uh, uh, my sun, my sun,' she was agitated and wriggled awkwardly to regain the afternoon glare.

'It's not *your* sun,' I reminded her.

'Just move.'

I stood aside and carefully rested my board against the rocks. 'You going in?'

Mel looked up at me and slowly lowered her sunnies to reveal a patronising look.

'Why not? It's perfect — hot weather, calm water. What's your problem?'

With sunnies still drawn down, Mel turned her gaze across the sand. Amanda Wellings was sunning herself like a skinny little rock lizard in a skimpy bikini.

'Mel — you've got to stop with this crap. She's a Beach Rat. You can't avoid them.'

Beach Rats are like parasites that live on the sand dunes. They are of anorexic build and usually travel in packs, probably to give themselves some sense of size. Seeing one on its own is rare.

'Skinny cow.' Mel pushed her glasses back into place and turned to me. 'Ready to go?'

We gathered our gear and walked up the hill.

'Seriously, Jonah,' Mel said, recovering from her Beach Rat phobia, 'you do look different. You've gotten a lot bigger.'

'You sound like Mum. I started weight training while I was up with Link. It fully changes your body, hey?'

'Maybe I should do it too.' Mel lifted her t-shirt and sucked in her stomach.

'Oh stop with this chick-shit, would you? You're fat and you know it.'

She swung her beach bag in a wide angle and belted me hard across the back. The thing was, Mel had shape: boobs that actually filled out her tops, occasional cleavage and a nice round bum. Next to the flat-tack Beach Rats, she was a woman.

'So what'd you want to tell me?' I stopped at the top of the hill to put on my t-shirt.

'What?'

'You know.'

'What?'

'You know, Mel.' I picked up my board. 'On the phone this week. Something to tell me? Wanting to talk?'

'Oh, that.'

'Yeah, that.' We continued to walk, rounding the curves of the Rotary track. 'So,' I insisted, 'just say it.'

She stopped walking and looked at me, her eyes locking with mine. And suddenly I felt something ignite inside me — a funny little flame that had never been there before.

'Well ...' She took a deep breath.

'Hi, Jonah!' It was like hearing the alarm when you're in deep sleep. I turned to see Amanda jogging behind us. 'You're back. You look fantastic. Have you been working out?' She gripped my bicep and I smiled proudly.

'Hi, Mel.' Amanda did one of those stupid little finger ripples. Mel returned the wave before pretending to vomit behind Amanda's back.

'You look awesome, Jonah,' Amanda gushed. 'No joke. You could be like twenty-one or something. And your skin looks good too.' I rubbed at my chin and thought of Link carefully teaching me how to shave.

We walked all the way back to Lakeview Avenue with Amanda chattering nonstop. Mel plodded along beside her and almost snorted when Amanda said she hadn't recognised me on the beach.

Mel didn't speak, even when we reached her house. She stomped up the steps and slammed the door. I was left with Amanda who was still talking, following me right to my house and even up my driveway. She kept going on about people from school and saying how good I looked. Eventually, I gave her one of those little finger-wiggle waves and left her standing there.

Safe inside, I headed for the bathroom. I studied myself in the mirror and tried to see the changes everyone else was noticing. My skin was heaps better. Link's three-step treatments had seen to that. I flexed my biceps and drew in my stomach. My arms were bigger and my torso was angular. I suppose I had bulked up. It felt good.

I did a few more poses, then let my body hang limp. Relaxed like that, with my gut jutting out and my shoulders all slumped, I looked more like I was five. I tensed up for another pose, trying to imagine how old I could look. Maybe twenty, I thought. Twenty-two at a stretch.

I slumped again and pulled a face at my reflection. Salt had crusted to my cheek, like a dry white dust. I angled out my tongue and licked it off.

The last Saturday of the summer holidays is always bittersweet. You've got the memories of what was and the dread of what's to come. Ferret, Dan and I were silent as we trudged over the Rotary track to Bar looking for some early-morning adrenaline. Dan had assured me that the Bar had been going off this summer and our last moments of holiday should be devoted to the place, worshipping what the gods had delivered.

Sure enough, the swell was good and the sets were regular. Dan had the place sussed, knowing exactly where the sand bar fell and precisely where to wait. By comparison I felt as though I was fumbling. My weeks in Canberra shadowed behind me like a torturous punishment and I wondered if I'd ever surf properly again. I was grateful for Ferret, blundering among us as usual. He had his full snorkel mask, wetsuit, fins and boogie board. He struggled to get onto anything.

As the tourists settled onto the beach and the late-morning punters dropped in on us, I finally found some form. Sliding down a slow-moving mountain that threatened to drop me at any minute, I hoped to God that Dan was watching. I could hear Ferret hooting behind me, just audible above the churning of the wave. I caught three more after that, gaining confidence with each ride.

We sat on the beach for a while, drying out in the blazing sun. Ferret had bought hot donuts from the van and we burnt our tongues choking them down. They were the ultimate summer breakfast.

'So have you been on the 'roids or what?' The question steamed out of Dan as he juggled a scalding piece of donut in his mouth.

'Nah, you loser. I've been doing weights. Eating right. You know the sort of stuff you do when you go to uni.'

'Oh man,' Ferret looked disappointed. 'I thought you just shagged women and smoked dope.'

'Yeah — that too.' I grabbed the bag of donuts and took the last one.

'As if you've shagged a woman.' Ferret's eyes remained on the waves.

'I did. Every night.'

Ferret turned, his expression sceptical.

'Ah, stop it Jonah.' Dan swiped the back of Ferret's head and pulled a face at him. 'He hasn't screwed a woman. Don't panic.'

'Yeah, I knew it.' Ferret turned back to the surf, folding his arms tight across his chest.

'Weights, you reckon?' Dan interrogated me and I tried to stay cool. Lifting weights wasn't rocket science, but I wanted to own it for a while.

We walked up the hill to Short Point Beach, knowing the waves would be crap. Short was the place to go though; more space, more girls. As we walked, the lads drilled me about my weeks in Canberra.

'Any Sirens?' Ferret asked as we passed the Caravan Park his parents owned.

'Are you still talking that crap?'

'He'll be talking that crap till he dies,' said Dan.

Sirens had become Ferret's code word for beautiful

women. Years ago in primary school, before he'd discovered internet porn, Ferret had found his folks' old video and DVD collection. It was extensive, including all the ex-rentals they'd offered at the Caravan Shop. There was one called *Sirens* starring Elle Macpherson and Kate Fischer. It was rated MA and Ferret was certain it would be hot stuff. During a sleepover, the three of us had watched it at midnight, fast-forwarding endless scenes trying to find the sex and tits Ferret had promised. It turned out to be a period drama set in the twenties or something. The entire film had only a few minutes of nudity and no sex. We did see Elle's boobs, for a moment. Ferret put them on pause, but it wasn't quite the same.

'Nuh. There were no Sirens.' A vision of Katerina came into my mind. I didn't want to share her with Ferret. 'If there were Sirens, I couldn't see them anyway. I had my eyes closed rooting women every night.'

'You peckerhead,' Ferret said in a patronising tone. 'You don't close your eyes while you're having a root.'

'What would you know, you little virgin?'

'Stop it, you freaks.' Dan never engaged in this sexual warfare. Word on the street was that he and Stacey had been doing the deed for years. It was another useless piece of chick-shit Mel had thrown my way during Year 11.

'Well, there's Sirens galore at the Park right now,' Ferret said. 'They're just strolling around the place like you could buy them from the two-dollar shop. Hot as anything.'

I laughed at him and shook my head.

We were at the Point, with the Pacific Ocean stretched before us. The beach was bright and colourful, packed with sunburnt tourists on faded towels. Little kids were having adventures in the nearby lake that sometimes opened to the sea. The delicious smell of hot chips gradually turned to the bitter scent of sunscreen as we scrambled down the rocks to the sand.

The waves were scrappy and crowded; even over towards Tura there were nasty little rips and messy sets. The punters were doing their worst, turning the few good waves into car wrecks with their shiny new boards and inexperienced efforts. We settled on the sand near the rock pools, bagging out the try-hards and eyeing off the chicks. Ferret went in for a bit before getting booted out by the lifeguards. He was riding his board like a maniac, dropping in on little kids and annoying the crap out of everyone between the flags.

After twelve, the Beach Rats arrived. They were like a school of tiny fish, travelling in the slipstream of their mighty leader, Stacey Holland. She was Dan's girlfriend — had been since the start of Year 9. She was in the year below us and was hot property. Dan had laid claim.

The Rats settled around us, trying to look casual

even though they'd just spent hours dressing for the beach. Stacey gave Dan a kiss that bordered on X-rated.

There was some mindless conversation: relentless bitching about other girls on the beach and gossip about people from school. Ferret fuelled things along, adding his usual comments, which had the Rats squealing and screwing up their glossy faces.

'Do we have to sit *here*?' one of the Rats appealed to Stacey, rolling her eyes after a disgusting comment from Ferret.

'Only till the wind comes up.' Ferret was quick. 'Then you'll all have to move 'cause your bikini tops'll be flapping in the breeze. The noise is distracting.'

Stacey gave Dan a look. It was the sort of look wives give to husbands and I wondered if she'd read about it in *Cleo* or something. Surely there was a manual where girls learnt these tricks.

'Time for a surf.' Dan was on the move before Stacey could protest.

Ferret leapt up and I realised this was Dan's way of solving the Rats' problem. He must've been reading *Cleo* too, or some other specialist book that couples knew about.

Messy waves don't always equate to bad surfing. Dan and I established a reasonable position out the back, nodding to locals and cutting off punters, as protocol dictated. The rides were okay. There was lots of foam, and whitewash kept bubbling off the waves causing them to break haphazardly rather than in one long piece.

'Crumblers,' Ferret shouted at me from under his snorkel mask. I nodded and shrugged. Dan was messing about, practising turns and hardly riding the waves through at all. I started experimenting myself, taking late drops and turning hard before launching off in crazy dives. Ferret was having fun too, bouncing around on his boogie board and trying to stand up. His flippers made everything awkward and the board kept hitting him on the head.

'Hey Dan, look what's on the menu.' I flicked my head towards some thickening sets that were approaching. The surf was shaping up and we were right on the mark. Dan hooted and paddled out beside me. We watched the swell curl in and planned our attack.

Dan went first, pumping along the wave with a lust that rivalled the kiss he gave Stacey. He turned sharply, grinding into it and demanding more. I watched enviously; he'd gained a lot this summer and I knew I'd been left behind.

I pulled out of the next wave. It was covered with punters like flies on a turd. Swearing, I paddled out further, trying to re-establish my place in the line-up.

I caught the last of the set. It was fast and steep and I stayed low before turning hard just as Dan had done. I smashed the lip, suspended for a moment before landing it. I let the wave take me, enjoying the ride until it petered out and I jumped off into the whitewater. My pulse was racing and I couldn't stop smiling. A good wave was magic.

Ferret was on the shore as I paddled in. Glancing back, I saw Dan following me. Our one perfect set had been the ocean's gift. The crumblers had returned.

I walked along the sand, inspecting my board and chipping at a nub of wax. Ferret was watching someone and I followed his gaze. A woman was strolling through the shallows. It was like one of those scenes from a James Bond movie. She came out of the surf as though it was her home, calm and steady. Her hair was dark and slicked back and she moved like the world would wait for her.

Standing with the boys, I watched her emerge. Her bikini was a skimpy cut and I could see that every curve was faultless. She was like something golden. Something perfect.

'Now that is a Siren,' said Dan in a reverent whisper.

Ferret nodded, his eyes focused in silent worship.

The woman reached behind her neck and drew her hair over her shoulder. She squeezed the strands tightly, dragging her fists down the entire length. A tiny river of water trickled between her breasts.

'Oh, yes,' whispered Ferret.

She walked towards us and I shifted my board uncomfortably, sensing that an unwanted erection might suddenly arrive.

'She's coming to us,' Ferret said. 'We've caught a Siren, fellas. We've caught a Siren.'

Her beauty was amazing. As she came closer I could see the slightest hint of sunburn stained across her shoulders.

'Hey,' she said as she approached. 'Nice moves out there.'

We stared back at her, hypnotised.

'Yeah,' Dan grunted.

'Thanks,' Ferret's courage built on Dan's initiative. He pulled at his snorkel mask, which was perched on his forehead. The rubber straps made a smacking sound.

'I like the way you surf,' the Siren said. She had positioned her body at an angle, blocking Dan and Ferret. She was speaking to me. I tried to think of something to say. I had nothing.

'I taught him all he knows,' Ferret said. 'You're staying at the Park, aren't you?' He nodded towards the Caravan Park on the hill.

'Yeah,' she glanced at Ferret nodding. 'You?'

'Nah, we live round here.' Ferret was natural; as though he spoke to beautiful women every day. 'My folks own the Park. I think I saw you there.'

She made a little noise, kind of like 'oh' or 'hmm'. I couldn't tell. It was as if she had me on pause, her finger stuck right on the button.

'Come round for a drink tonight. I'm in the back row.' She pointed suddenly, gesturing towards the vans that overlooked Long Point. 'It's the third van along.' Her arm was out and I could see the roundness of her left breast and the rigid hardness of her nipple, pointing out to sea.

'Seven o'clock?' Her tone was so suggestive and my body strung so tight, I couldn't even manage to look her in the eyes.

'Sounds fun, hey Jonah?' Dan nudged me. 'Seven, yeah.' He nodded with his usual confidence and I tried to dredge up some pride of my own. I risked a look at her face and found her eyes, big and green and wide, seeking mine. They looked into me and I was certain she would see that I was really Feet. Just seventeen, a virgin and pretty much a dickhead too. She smiled at me, a slow gift that spread across her face, revealing a friendliness that lay beneath the sheen of glamour.

'Okay then, see you.' She walked away from us and we watched in silence. Eventually she stopped, bending over for her towel. Ferret groaned and grabbed at his crotch.

'You idiot.' Dan slapped the back of Ferret's head as the Siren turned around. Ferret adjusted his boogie board, shielding his groin. Suddenly, she raised her arm in a wave and began jogging back towards us.

'Oh yes, oh yes,' Ferret panted, as her tits moved in time with her stride.

'Sorry,' she laughed, towelling at her hair. 'I'm Amity by the way. See you at seven, Jonah.' She left again, jogging back to her friends on the beach. I couldn't watch though, I had to turn away. Looking at her was like staring at the sun. After a while, it hurt your eyes.

'You choked, Jonah,' Ferret laughed, bringing us back to reality. 'Absolutely choked!'

We left the beach without the Rats. We'd forgotten about them. We walked without speaking and were almost halfway up the hill to the Caravan Park before Dan even remembered Stacey.

'Damn! I didn't tell Stace we were leaving.'

'Who?' Ferret stopped and turned to Dan. 'Oh,' he said sarcastically, 'that piece of fish bait you keep dangling on your line? Yeah, I remember. The fifteen-year-old. We don't need her, mate. Jonah's bagged us a Siren.'

'She's not a Siren.' It was the first time I had spoken since leaving the water.

'Yeah, she is. She came for you. You called her from the sea with that goofy surfing and those pumped-up biceps. You two are going to bang tonight.' Ferret thrust his pelvis and moaned.

'Can you believe that just happened?' I shook my head and kept walking.

'It happened,' Ferret insisted. 'I've got the hard-on to prove it.'

'Shut up,' Dan said. 'We don't want to hear about your little pecker.'

'But, she's like twenty-five or something.' I kept my head down.

'Don't ask questions,' Dan said. 'You're in. Go

for it.'

'She invited us *all*.' Ferret looked up at Dan, who shook his head.

'Nuh, she's Jonah's. He bagged her, she's his.'

'I didn't bag her.' My voice was strung out. I was panicking. What would I do with her? With a woman?

'Don't you get it?' Ferret turned, swiping my surfboard with his little red boogie. 'You walk around here with those big muscles and new clothes. Geez, mate, I've had a hard time not cracking onto you myself.'

We followed Ferret through the Park entrance and hosed off our boards.

'Hey,' said Dan as though a thought had just occurred, 'Stacey's not fish bait, you pervert.' He turned the hose on Ferret who screamed like a girl and ran.

3

At 6.50 I walked back through the Park entrance. Ferret was waiting to meet me and I was relieved.

'Nice,' he said, scanning me up and down.

I was wearing a Canberra Clothes outfit: collared t-shirt, cargo pants *and* shoes. Link had taught me well.

'Here,' Ferret offered me a fistful of something and I reached out to take it.

'Oh, you loser,' I said as the tiny condom packets slipped from my hand. 'How many did you think I'd need anyway?'

'Well, there's twelve there.' Ferret was serious.

I wanted to laugh at him, but I also wanted to listen. Was I about to have sex for the first time? For the first twelve times? I had put two condoms in my wallet, both of them taken from a packet I had stolen in Link's flat. I didn't even know *how* to have sex. Not really, not the way I'd seen on movies or on Ferret's internet sites.

'Twelve? Who do you think I am?' I thought of the poster of the black man. He had the equipment for twelve. I had a drinking straw in comparison.

'You're so lucky,' Ferret said. 'You always get the

good ones.'

I grinned at Ferret's envy, but knew it was founded on lies. During the last inter-school sports visit, I had been billeted out with a girl called Lindsay. My teachers had thought it was a boy's name and so had I. But I was buddied up with a gorgeous blonde who had a nice set of curves hidden beneath her school jumper. I didn't bother to tell my teachers.

Lindsay and I had had a lot of fun together. We'd pashed our way through the school social and she'd let me have a decent sample of her tits. But she had a disabled brother at home and made it clear that her parents didn't need the hassle of finding their daughter in bed with the billet.

During the bus ride back to school everyone just assumed I'd had sex with Lindsay. I had followed Dan's lead, saying nothing. Eventually it just became inter-school sports folklore and I never bothered to set the record straight. It was coming back to haunt me now. Ferret thought I knew what I was doing.

We stopped in front of the caravan. I was sweating. My penis was all shrivelled up, hiding among my pubes. I felt like a soldier advancing out on the front line. Relax, I thought. Pretend you're Link. Just be Link.

At the door I paused and realised I was still holding a handful of condoms. I shoved them hastily into the various pockets of the cargos. Then, before I could back out, Ferret stepped forward, knocked on the door and ran off.

My heart went into a sprint when I saw Amity. For a moment she was framed in the shabby caravan doorway like a supermodel. She was wearing a skirt and a t-shirt. Her nipples were hard and seemed to be staring at me, recognising me for the nervous youngster that I was. She stepped down and kissed my cheek, her tits pressing against me. My dick was up for the challenge. It was out from the pubes and well on its way to full mast.

Amity had been speaking, but I'd been listening to my dick. My brain was only now kicking in.

'I was just going to sit outside,' she was saying. 'I'm a bit sunburnt and I can't get comfortable. One minute I'm hot and the next I'm freezing.' She gave a little shiver and grabbed a jacket from the van. She turned back and was again framed in the doorway. I still hadn't moved, except for my dick, which was trying to get into the van all on its own.

'Take a seat,' Amity gestured to the outdoor chairs. I sat gratefully, knowing my hard-on wouldn't be so obvious. Amity stepped back inside and returned with two beers. She passed one to me and I quickly removed the top, hoping I looked casual and experienced.

She sat opposite me, her tits now covered by the fleecy jacket. I hadn't noticed her legs before. They were long and smooth and brown. She crossed them and where her thighs pressed together, a line formed like leg cleavage. I tried not to stare.

I sucked at the beer, drinking down a good

third of it. It was icy cold and bristled my throat. I squashed the cap in my other hand, working it into a tight little cylinder. My heart was hammering out of my chest, I could even feel my pulse thundering beneath my skin.

'Do you surf?' I'd thought of the question as I was dressing for the date. I didn't want to seem as hopeless as I had on the beach.

'Me?' she laughed. 'Nah, not really. Always wanted to.'

'I could teach you.'

She smiled and I felt myself blush. Amity pressed her beer bottle down against her thigh. It left a round wet imprint on her leg.

'So ... Where are your friends?' Amity took a sip of beer and tugged her sleeves down in that girly way, so only her fingers were poking out.

'Work.' I was pleased that she'd asked. The boys and I had rehearsed this question too.

'Oh yeah, where do they work?'

I was stunned, unprepared. None of us had jobs, not real ones anyway.

'Um, McDonalds.' Even to me, it sounded like I was guessing.

'Jonah,' Amity leant forward and I could smell something sweet, 'how old are you?'

'Twenty.' I said it quickly, taking another long drink of beer. I sucked at it too hard and as I drew the bottle away it stuck to my mouth, stretching my lip with the intensity of a vacuum. I yanked the bottle loose with a loud shlucking noise.

'Really?'

I looked at her, from her cute little feet right up to her leg cleavage and big tits. Her eyes were drilling into me under eyebrows raised up like umbrellas. Her entire face was a question mark and I was pretty sure she already knew the answer.

'I'm seventeen,' I sighed. 'Eighteen in August.' My tone was hopeful and she smiled.

'Seventeen,' she sort of breathed the number out between her teeth and gave me a thorough going-over with those gorgeous eyes. 'Well you had me. Oh, God!' She threw her head back and covered her face with her hands. 'Seventeen!'

'Yeah, well it sounds young when you say it like that, but I mean, it's seventeen. I've got my Ps. I don't have a car but …'

Amity laughed, throwing her head back to let the sound escape. She was beautiful.

'Oh, Jonah.' And something changed. The dynamics shifted and it was like I was with Kat again. Just friends.

'Why do you say "Oh, Jonah" like that? Like you feel sorry for me?' I looked down at my feet.

'Oh,' she sighed and apologised. 'You're seventeen. I'm twenty-six. That's —'

'Nine years. I know. I'm not stupid.' Knowing I sounded like a kid.

'Hey,' she drew her chair close and put her hand on my leg, 'don't take it personally.' She rubbed her

45

hand up and down and just when I felt there was hope, she reached up and ruffled my hair. 'You're a cutie though!' She pinched my cheek, like I was five years old.

'So what now?' I drank my beer carefully.

'Well — we hang out and talk. If you still want?'

I shrugged. I didn't want to talk. I'd had enough talking with Katerina. I wanted more.

She stepped into the van and returned wearing tracksuit pants and smelling of Aeroguard. She dropped another beer onto my lap and settled down into her chair.

Just like Kat, she talked on and on about her life, her dreams, her goals, her fears. It was like an essay called chick-shit and each topic had a subheading. She was nice though, and interesting. She'd travelled a bit and was now studying psychology in Melbourne. She'd grown up in Eden, which was just half an hour up the road.

'My folks have left Eden now. They've got a few acres out at Cuttagee,' she explained. 'It's right on the beach and it's beautiful, but there's no night-life, no people. I like to stay here for a bit, makes it feel like a real holiday. Plus, I sometimes catch up with friends from around here.'

We did the usual small-town connections, finding our six degrees of separation. It turned out she knew of Link.

'He's a great surfer, isn't he? He was a few years

below me at school. But he went to St Peter's right?' She yawned and I took it as my cue.

I stood up and felt the condoms sink down in my pockets. There was an awkward moment and I wished I hadn't tried so hard. The stupid clothes, the after-shave and the hair gel; she knew now that I was trying to act older, that everything about me was a lie. I scuffed my shoe against the asphalt.

Amity stepped forward and kissed me. She leant in and pressed her beautiful face against mine, her lips melting my mouth and covering me. My heart thundered and I could hear the ocean, just metres away, rhythmically washing against the sand. My dick strained against my jocks, nudging it's way up under my belt.

'I'm sorry, Jonah,' she said, drawing away and holding my hand. 'I really am.'

It was a sympathy kiss and I knew I was meant to be grateful; to take it with me like a gift. A souvenir of our time together.

'I'm coming back next weekend.' She smiled. 'Call round.'

My body was wound up tight as I left the Park and my dick was still standing to attention, but I felt like crap. I considered calling in at Ferret's but I wasn't ready for the shame. I was desperate for a surf but it was dark and late. I couldn't be bothered with the hassle of trying to sneak my board out of the garage and walking all the way back up to the Point.

There were no lights on at Mel's, so I continued home. When I got in, I sent Mel a text. I waited, but there was no reply. I stripped off my Canberra Clothes and fell into bed.

'Mornin' lads,' Dan paddled out to meet Ferret and me. It was early Sunday morning — the last day of summer holidays. We were on the bar and the sets had been slow but consistent.

'Alright, Dan's here. Tell us everything.' Ferret sat up on his boogie board, like it was an eight-foot Mal.

'Nothing to tell.' I stared out to sea.

'Just tell us.' Dan slapped his hand against the water. We were the only three out there and I longed for a distraction. A wave, a punter, even a shark. Anything to avoid telling them about last night.

'How was she?' Ferret's tongue was hanging out. 'Did you put your head between those kahoonas and just suffocate yourself?' He mimed out his little fantasy, shaking his head from side to side and blowing raspberries.

'No.' I swivelled my board around, watching the water swirl with my current. I thought about lying, decided not to. 'We're just friends. I didn't sleep with her.'

'*Friends*?' Ferret was exploding. '*Sleep* with her? You're not meant to sleep with her; you're meant to root her. Friends? I'm your friend. Tits like that aren't looking for friends.'

Dan reached out and yanked Ferret's arm rope. Ferret toppled over, flippered feet still gripping onto his stubby board.

I looked at Dan and he shrugged.

'It's just sex.' He was cool. 'Don't stress about it.'

Ferret surfaced blowing hard into his snorkel. 'You're a disgrace, Jonah. I wouldn't even go home to my own family after that.'

'You're such a virgin, Ferret — so desperate.' Dan shook his head.

'I am not.' Ferret was outraged. 'I had sex last night.'

'Yeah, but shagging your mum doesn't count.'

I laughed and paddled out to catch a wave.

That afternoon I caught up with Mel. We drew up a study timetable and reviewed notes from last year. The dark cloud of Year 12 loomed closer: thicker and meaner than ever before.

'What're you going to do next year?' Mel was lying on the floor, her feet pointing and flexing at random.

'Dunno.' I twisted my head to each side, waiting for the satisfying crack. 'I still dunno.'

'I don't think I'll go to uni.' She pointed both feet out straight.

'Yeah, you will.'

'Maybe not.' Her feet flexed.

I stretched out my legs, letting my feet press

against hers. She kicked against me and we wrestled for a moment, our legs tangling together in an uncomfortable heap.

'I had a date last night,' I said.

'Yeah, I know.'

'Who told you?'

'Ferret. Said you crashed and burned.'

'I didn't crash and burn. I made a friend. You should be proud of me.'

Mel snorted. 'Yeah, I'm proud. I'll present the trophy later!' She rolled onto her side and started piling up books. 'See you tomorrow.'

I went with her to the door and then kept going, walking her up the street to her house. I didn't carry the books though; I wanted to punish her for talking with Ferret. Mel didn't care. I don't think she even noticed. At her front door she asked if I'd be needing a flag as well.

'A flag?'

'Yeah, and the national anthem played when you get your big trophy for making a friend.'

I stuck out my tongue and pulled a face.

'Good comeback,' she replied quickly. 'I'll see you on the dais, Trophy Boy.'

4

My first day of Year 12 — my last 'first day back at school' — began with a painful photo opportunity at the front door. Every year Mum had me stand in the same place with my uniform all ironed and clean. I posed and smiled, trying hard not to grimace. Mum flicked the camera around, showing me the image on screen. She zoomed in, bringing my face up large. Next to my head was a framed picture Link had done as a kid. It featured me, drawn in crayon; an overweight stick figure with green hair and purple eyes. FEET was printed in large random letters above the picture. It annoyed me, even though I'd never really noticed it before.

'Take that down,' I turned and nudged the frame.

'No, I like it.' Mum frowned and re-positioned it carefully.

'It's crap.'

'Jonah!'

I shrugged and hauled up my backpack. Mum kissed me and touched my face.

'Have a good day, hey? You're nearly finished.'

'Yeah. Nearly finished.'

St Peter's Secondary College is in the tiny town of Pambula, a thirty-minute bus ride from my house. It has an ancient front façade as though the place grew there, rising up from the depths of the earth. It was founded in 1864 by nuns and priests that have long since become extinct.

The school emblem is carved into the front entrance. *Ingredior Per Fides*. Walk with faith. It's meant to remind us of St Peter, the fisherman who walked on water to meet Jesus. Supposedly Peter grew to have great faith, but he had it easy, really. Being best friends with Jesus Christ couldn't have been that difficult. Imagine what Jesus could do with HSC results if he could turn water into wine. The Bible makes St Peter's life sound tough: all that fishing and preaching. But Peter didn't have to do the HSC. Walk with faith — I needed more than faith. Some exam answers could be handy, or a guarantee of what I might do with my life.

Ferret staggered along next to me, weighed down by his backpack. Dan strolled beside him with Stacey trailing off his arm. I could hear the Beach Rats gossiping in her wake. I looked around for Mel, who hadn't been on the bus.

The school seemed empty with only the seniors and Year 7s attending the first day. We hung out in our usual area, watching as the Year 7s studied timetables and scuffed their new shoes. Ferret gave each girl a score as she went past, earning a bitchy look from Stacey.

By 9.15 it felt as though we'd never been away. Pastoral care had been a short welcome and then a massive list of dates and details about trials, exams and school masses. I couldn't believe the teachers were assuming we'd survive the year. I thought of Link and Katerina and their skanky flat. My uni days seemed like a distant dream.

We followed the same timetable as the previous year. Our lessons resumed as though the past six weeks hadn't happened. By recess my hand was sore from writing and my brain was frying in its own juices. It was good to get outside again.

'Late bus?' Dan asked as we met up.

'Shit yeah,' I said. Ferret nodded.

St Peter's was just up the road from Pambula Beach. It was a pretty inconsistent place for surfing, but it was something. We often headed down for a quick surf straight after school and caught the 5.00 p.m. bus home. We kept our old boards in the sheds at the Surf Club and if we were ever really desperate, we wagged class and went for a hit.

'God, I could do with a fix right now.' Ferret sprawled on the grass, in the shade of the big eucalypt we had claimed as our own since Year 7. 'Bloody Johnston. I don't know why I ever thought I could do advanced maths with him breathing down my neck. He's got it in for me.'

I plucked at the hairs on my legs, envious of Ferret. He was an absolute Einstein with numbers. His future in the real world was guaranteed.

'Why didn't I get Mrs Dialto? She's funny and she's got nice tits.'

'Because she teaches food technology, you nuff-nuff.' Dan belted Ferret on the head before reaching up a hand to Stacey who had just arrived.

'Has anyone seen Mel?' I shielded my eyes from the glare and scanned the playground. Ferret shrugged and Dan slurped as he devoured Stacey.

The rest of the day passed in a haze of classes, assignments, note-taking and problem-solving. The last lesson was Catholic Studies; a religion subject was compulsory at St Peter's for all students from Years 7 to 12. Ms Finlay was the one reason that the entire class turned up. She was young and attractive. Dan said she had great tits, although Ferret argued there was no such thing as a bad set. She wore tight-fitting clothes and short skirts. Ms Finlay was a package deal. She was nice too, the sort of teacher who didn't get on your back about trivial stuff.

'Okay — Year 12. You made it.' Ms Finlay gave us a little round of applause and a warm smile. I could see Ferret sitting in the front row, angling for a perve down her shirt.

'Now,' she studied a piece of paper and glanced at us, 'it seems we'll be meeting three times a week. I can't wait. Most exciting is Friday period 6.' There were groans from everyone. Catholic Studies was valuable time chewed up by a crap subject. It was all about serving the community and making the world a better place. Period 6 on a Friday was just a ploy to keep us on the school grounds. At St Peter's poor attendance meant you didn't get a reference. And no invitation to the formal either.

'Hang on,' Ms Finlay continued. 'I'm happy to let you use that time for study of something other than Catholic Studies. I thought we could spend some time getting sorted out. For the future.' She held up a large cardboard carton. There was a hole cut in the top, like a letterbox. 'Any question. Any concern. Write it down, drop it in. We'll talk about it on Friday. It's anonymous and it's for you guys. What do you think?'

'Can we ask stuff about sex?' Ferret was straight to the point.

The girl next to Ferret smirked. 'You mean like remedial work for virgins?'

'Nah, like specific stuff.' Ferret shrugged. 'Like oral sex.'

'Now what would you need to know about oral sex?' Ms Finlay sat on the edge of Ferret's desk. She was a lioness, about to go in for the kill. 'I understand you're already the master of it. I mean — you talk about it all day long. Isn't that "oral sex"?'

The class laughed and even Ferret cracked a smile.

'Right,' she said, smoothing down her shirt. 'Let's begin with a prayer.'

I sent Mel a text that night but got no reply. I felt overwhelmed by the year ahead, and surfing that afternoon hadn't helped. I had only caught three good waves and the rest had been crap. There were still tourists everywhere and on my last wave, a young girl had dropped in on me.

Over the dinner table, Mum's usual interrogations began.

'How was school?'

'Okay.'

'What's your timetable like?'

'Same.'

'How're your friends?'

'Okay.'

'Are you even listening to me?'

'Are you listening to me? I don't want to talk.' I shovelled in some food and felt guilty. Without losing a beat, Dad handed Mum a pile of mail.

Mum ruffled through the papers as we ate in silence. She flicked savagely through a Best & Less catalogue before resuming her attack. 'Between you and Link I don't know what's going on. Apparently I'm just an incubator — good for nine months and then that's it.' She flicked another flimsy page, revealing headless jock shots. I thought of Link and wondered if his modelling had expanded to include the latest undies sold at Best & Less.

'Mum,' I stood up and kissed her on the top of her head, 'you're closer to us than you think. They're nice, don't you reckon?' I pointed at some beige Y-fronts and left the table.

Link rang later that night, checking up on my

first day.

'Are you still running?' he asked.

'I don't have time for running. I've got a million subjects and the pressure of exams. If I've got spare time, I'm surfing.'

'Get up earlier, Feet, and go for a run. You'll feel better. How's Mum?'

'Freaking out. She knows something's up with you. She's on my back about everything. Just tell her, will you?'

'No. And don't you say anything, Feet.'

'Whatever. Hey, I went for a date with a twenty-six-year-old.'

'You did not.' Link was dismissive.

'Did so. Amity Pender. You might even know her, she —'

'You did not.' There was a laugh in Link's voice. Disbelief.

'I did. I'm seeing her again this weekend.'

'Bull.'

'So, you know her?'

'Yeah I —' Link stopped. 'You're full of it. Let me talk to Mum. And don't say anything, or I'll come down there and wring your scrawny little pecker off its hinges.'

Mel didn't come to school until Wednesday. By then, all grades were attending and the place was like a metropolis.

'Where've you been?'

'Busy.' Mel spoke quietly to the English teacher, took her allocated texts and sat down next to me.

'Busy with Ferret?'

'What?' Her folder was open and she squeezed the rings shut with a snap.

'You've been talking to him a lot.'

'So?'

'So.' I frowned, trying to work out what I wanted to say.

'I'll talk to you later, Jonah. I can't do this right now, okay?' Her face was soft. Sad. I didn't want to upset her. Not Mel.

'Yeah, okay.'

At recess, we met at our usual hangout. I tried to get a quiet moment alone with Mel, but Ferret was going berserk. A new group had settled near us: Year 7 girls who were too young and innocent to know any better. Ferret was calling out, giving them scores and a comment.

'Full of potential,' he yelled. 'Nice butt, nice hair. Shame about your tits. I'll give you a six.'

'Give it a rest,' Mel dragged her lunch box from her bag and tossed her drink bottle at Ferret.

'Hey, steady on.' He threw the bottle back at Mel and I watched them carefully. Mel gave him a smile and Ferret winked. I looked away.

'Hey!' Ferret stood up, pointing wildly. 'There she is. Jumper Girl. She's back. I knew she'd be back. Oh, Jumper Girl!' He gestured to a girl walking across the quad. As usual, she had her jumper on, even though it was thirty degrees in the shade. Ferret had christened her Jumper Girl when she arrived late last year. She always wore her school jumper, even down the street. Ferret was fascinated.

'I've got a new theory about her.' He sat down and opened a packet of chips. 'Body art. You know, freakish tattoos all over her like someone off *Ripley's Believe It Or Not.*'

'You've got to give up,' Dan said. 'Just get over her.'

'I can't.' Ferret looked forlorn. 'It's like I've got a fetish for her. A fetish for a girl with a jumper fetish. Do you think there's a special name for that kind of fetish?'

'Shut up, Ferret,' Dan said. Stacey was hanging out with the Beach Rats and Dan had chemistry books stacked around him.

'Studying already?' Ferret dropped chip crumbs over Dan's work as he leant towards him. 'You've got bigger stuff to deal with than chemistry right now.'

'Like what?' Dan looked up, closing a textbook.

'Like Stacey's last name. If you marry her, she's going to have that whole double-barrel thing going on.'

Mel snorted as Ferret continued.

'I know we've covered this before, Dan, but since *your* name's Daniel Stacey, and her name *is* Stacey ... how's it going to work when you get hitched?'

Dan shook his head as we laughed. Stacey's first

name being the same as Dan's last had provided us with hours of amusement.

'I don't know what you see in her, Dan.' Mel's tone was gentle as the mood calmed. 'I mean, you're smart and funny and she's such a sheep.'

'Der, Mel!' Ferret opened another packet of chips, spilling half. 'It's the sex — sex on demand. Intelligent conversation's not on the agenda.'

'Hey,' Dan growled, 'Stacey's a nice person.'

Mel groaned.

'She is,' he insisted. 'She's just into different things. And she's deep.'

At that moment, Stacey rushed over. She was clutching a piece of paper and a purple gel pen.

'Guys!' Her eyes were shining as she thrust the paper in front of us. 'From now on I'm spelling my name like this.' She pointed to the page. 'See here, with an I-E. Not E-Y. S-T-A-C-I-E. Got it?'

We nodded, just holding it together until she left.

'She's deep,' Ferret said. 'Like a puddle.'

That night Mel and I walked to Short Point. I imagined her with Ferret, as a couple. A sick feeling flared inside me but I ignored it.

We scrambled down onto the rocks and settled on the ledge, hugged in by two large boulders. The ocean swelled beneath us, brimming and shrinking like something alive. Occasional sea spray wafted over us and I saw Mel turn her face towards it, soaking it up like a blessing.

She was pretty, with a round face and chubby cheeks. The body she was always complaining about was curvy and soft. Her hair was short and spiky, dyed in shades of blonde and brown. She looked at me and her eyes were dim and shadowed.

'It's Mum. The cancer. It's back.'

She leant into me and I held her, shuddering against me as though every part of her was crying.

I thought of Mel's mum: Merrin. Back in Year 6, she had nearly died. When it got bad, Mel had come to live with us. It was a screwed-up time, but Merrin had come good. In the January before we started high school, she pulled through. Went into remission. Never looked back.

Evening seeped over us and Mel drew away from me. She slapped her hands against her face, wiping away tears and hair and heartache. She was beautiful.

A silence opened up between us, filled by the ocean roaring and retreating. I waited for Mel to say more. Instead she looked at me, older than she'd been in Year 6. Wanting something. But I didn't know what.

'Are you seeing Ferret?'

'Fuck you, Jonah.' She was up and running before I could stop her, slipping over stones and scrambling up the cliff face. But her words kept coming back to me. Rolling in off the ocean.

I walked home alone, feeling like a low-life. *Are you seeing Ferret?* How stupid. No wonder Mel hadn't told me sooner. With a sick feeling, I remembered the phone calls in Canberra — the chick-shit. I kicked at a stone, booting it hard. I was a dickhead and well on my way to becoming a bastard.

I slammed through the house.

'Hey, keep it down. Your mother's in bed.' Dad was frowning as he watched me. 'What's wrong?'

'It's Merrin. The cancer's back.'

Dad nodded, looked at me. 'Are you alright, mate?'

It was what I should have asked Mel.

5

My phone woke me at 6.00. It was a text from Link.

go 4 a run

I rolled out of bed and was halfway up the hill before my body realised what I was doing. I continued up, punishing myself as I remembered last night. I started planning an apology, but everything sounded lame. The words *I'm sorry* thudded along with me, echoing my every step.

At home, Mum was serving up breakfast as Dad prepared for his shift. He checked his watch, ID, belt and badge. Mum was making tea, wringing the tea bag around the spoon. It was their usual routine but it made something shift inside me. I wondered who was making breakfast at Mel's house. I sat at the table, sweaty and exhausted.

'Where'd you go?' Dad reached for his tea.

'The Point and the wharf.'

'Be careful on that road back from the wharf.' Mum dropped bread into the toaster and expertly swivelled around for something from the fridge.

I started eating, while flicking through the local paper. Adverts, local council disputes, newborn babies and classifieds.

'Mel told you about Merrin?' Mum sat beside me.

I turned a page, thinking about what this meant. 'You knew?'

Mum nodded, a tiny tilt of her head. I shrugged, tried not to care.

'Mel wanted to tell you, Feet. We had to respect that.' She sipped her cuppa and eyeballed me. I read the paper. A quiet gent was seeking a female companion.

'Feet?'

'Whatever, Mum.' I shoved my chair out and left the room.

Mel was waiting for me at the end of my driveway. She was hugging her folder to her chest, like I'd seen her do a million times. It had never occurred to me that she was using it as a shield.

'Hey.'

'Hi.'

'I'm sorry. I thought ...'

'Yeah, I know.' Her voice was quick and sharp. She didn't want to talk. We walked down the hill and met a few of the others. The bus was late and Mel huddled next to me as a chilly summer mist blew in off the lake. But things weren't the same. I could tell. I had stuffed up majorly.

By Friday, everyone was hanging for the weekend. People were planning parties and even study sessions. Ferret was definitely in for the party scene and wanted me to go with him. Dan seemed intent on securing quality time with Stacey. He'd been groping her all through lunch and even Ferret had felt disgusted enough to tell them to get a room. I tried asking Mel what she had planned, but she didn't even look up from her book. Just shrugged and turned a page.

By period 6 I was dying for a surf and could've done with a smoke too. I hated fighting with Mel. Not that we were even fighting. She sat next to Ferret in Finlay's Catholic Studies class so I sat next to Amanda Wellings. Ferret was whispering something to Mel and she rolled her eyes at him. Amanda was telling me something too, but I couldn't be bothered listening.

Ms Finlay pulled a paper from the question box and turned to the whiteboard. In capital letters she wrote it up. *HOW DO I KNOW IF I'M DOING SEX RIGHT?* After the initial laughter, the class settled into silence and Ms Finlay shrugged.

'So?' She was wearing a tight white shirt. The buttons on her chest were only just holding it together. She was strolling around the room, probably trying to create a mood of curiosity and thoughtfulness. My dick was pretty curious — that was about all.

'How would you know?' She was out the front now. Gorgeous. 'How would you know if you'd gotten it wrong?'

'Well, it shouldn't be a pain in the arse.' Ferret, of

course. The whole class laughed. Even Finlay.

'Yes. But you're right too. It shouldn't be a pain. Sex should feel reasonably painless. What else?' She was walking around again. I could smell her perfume.

Eventually people started adding their own comments. How sex should be a mutual thing, have positive feelings, foreplay — especially important for girls, safer sex at all times. It was textbook stuff I already knew and didn't really help with my personal issue of how you actually got to the point of having sex.

After a while Ms Finlay took another question from the box. While she turned to write it on the board, Amanda slid her hand along my thigh. What with all the sexual tension Ms Finlay had created, it was enough to send my dick skyward. I looked down at her hand and saw every nail was a different colour — her index finger had been painted with liquid paper. I looked up at her face. She was like a white, starving Ethiopian. Amanda smiled at me and did something funny with her mouth. It was horror-porn stuff, but I didn't care. I was out of control, like I was fourteen all over again.

I shifted my leg, trying not to let her stroke too high. I didn't want her to know I had a massive boner. Talk about a rock and a hard place — I wanted to get laid for sure, but I sort of wanted to do it with someone I liked. Maybe that was my problem. I shifted my leg again, so Amanda couldn't quite reach. I smiled at her and looked at the board.

The question read: MS FINLAY, ARE YOU A VIRGIN? I could see Ferret watching her closely. I knew he'd written it, but I thought Finlay would have enough sense to censor the questions before the lesson. I looked at her and hoped she had a game plan.

She walked right up to Ferret's desk and perched neatly on the corner of it. She casually hooked her index finger into the V of her shirt and sort of tugged down. It was like a scene from some porno called *Hot Study Nights*. If sex appeal could drip, Ms Finlay was a fountain. Ferret looked like he might have been going to pass out. She leant towards him, giving him an eyeful of cleavage before standing up, facing the board and reading the question aloud.

'Ms Finlay, are you a virgin?' She turned back to face us. 'Well, only a virgin would ask that question. Wouldn't you agree? Michael?' Ferret shifted in his seat. He looked as though she had him by the balls. The look on her face said it all. She had gone from sex-on-a-stick to feminist-on-a-mission.

'In future, questions like that will result in a detention. Are we clear?'

'Yes, Ms Finlay.' Only Ferret answered. The rest of us tried not to laugh.

As we left the class, Amanda tried to hold my hand. I held hers for a moment but when Mel came out I let go, gripping my bag with both hands. I didn't know what the hell I was doing.

Waiting for the bus, I tried to make plans with Mel.

'I thought I might go see your mum.' I kicked at the ground, waited for her voice. 'Mel?'

'So go see her, Jonah. I'm going with Ferret. There's a party on.'

'Then I'll see you later?' I sounded desperate.

'Maybe.' She walked away from me and hopped into a car. Some idiot was driving and Ferret was in the back. He waved me over but I shook my head.

I walked up to Mel's wishing she was with me. Wishing she was with anyone but Ferret. I didn't want to see Merrin on my own, not now that she was sick. I tried to calculate how long the visit should last, how long I would have to stay without seeming rude. I wanted to surf and veg out and pretend things were okay. I didn't want to visit cancer.

'Jonah. Long time no see.' Merrin's voice was warm and genuine and the bastard feeling swelled inside me. 'Come and help me. I'm selling the Camry.'

She was at the table with newspapers and notebooks spread around her. Tiny spectacles were perched on her nose and she pulled them down, letting them hang from a chain around her neck. She looked happy and healthy and normal. Cancer was a fuck of a thing.

'The doctors say I won't be able to drive for much longer. I'll be having treatment and ...' she paused and rubbed fingers against thumbs, the sign for money. 'You remember how it was.' She gestured for me to sit down and I did. She ran a hand over my forehead and held my face. 'You're a handsome boy. You've really come into your own.'

She laughed as I let my head fall straight onto the table.

'Not you too,' I groaned. 'I spent a few weeks with Link and everyone thinks I've turned into him. I'm so different now and I've changed and blah blah blah.'

Merrin laughed again, her eyes lighting up. She poured me a drink and I read her ad. She was aiming for something quirky and interesting. It read like a poem.

'Your thoughts?'

'I like the rhyming and there's some nice sentimental imagery in there. But you haven't mentioned price or your phone number.'

'Listen to you — poetry appraisal. Spot the kid who's studying for his HSC.'

I let my head drop again.

'Okay. Okay.' Her hands went up in surrender. 'I should know better. Don't mention the H word. Mel's been driving me crazy.'

I sipped my drink and reread the poem.

'It's a shitty time, Jonah. But it'll pass.'

'I know.' I smiled at her and remembered to count my blessings.

My mobile had a message when I got home. It was from Amity. I flopped on my bed and read it through.

what u doing? come c me at the van. x x x.

I wanted to have some kind of dignity. I wanted to text back and say: *going for a surf you heartless bitch — you're too old for me anyway.* But I was still hoping she might want to screw me. I'd give her my virginity. She could have it, like some kind of keepsake for goddesses. I told Mum I was going to see Ferret and wandered up the hill.

Amity was sunbaking out the front of her van. She was listening to her iPod and didn't hear me coming. I took a moment to perve, staring at the way her tits slid a little to the side as she lay on her back. I wondered what they would feel like. She saw me and I had to end the fantasy in a hurry.

She stood up and stepped over to me, bubbling away with girly chat. She even leant forward and kissed my mouth, running her hands down my chest and touching the tiny school logo embroidered on the tie.

'I love a man in uniform.' She gave me a wicked smile and I knew I had to take a stand. My dick was going to poke her eyes out if I didn't put an end to things. Either that or I'd pass out from the sudden rushing of blood from brain to crotch. I reached for her and tried to kiss her again. She stepped back and eyed me suspiciously.

'So you just felt like being a tease?' I asked.

'I'm sorry.' She shut her eyes, shook her head. 'Bad habits.'

I shrugged, looked at her and waited.

'I want you to teach me to surf.' Her green eyes hopeful.

I hesitated. 'Alright.'

'Thank you, Jonah.' She squealed and hugged me, pressing against me as I tried to step back. 'Sorry.' She moved away, grabbed her towel. 'Sorry.'

'Meet me at Bar Beach. Twenty minutes.'

Bar was not a good place to learn surfing. It was out deep and you couldn't stand up. It was the best way to find potential and the fastest way to send the wannabes packing. But today, the swell was small and clean, exactly right for learning. After the day I'd had, I needed thumping, big, challenging rides. But I'd gone chasing my dick and hoping for sex. So here I was, pushing a wetsuited Amity along a wave and screaming at her to *stand up, stand up, stand up*.

She wasn't that bad and I was sure it wasn't her first time. She was a strong swimmer and managed to stay out for over an hour. Her timing was good but her movements were slow. She caught a few waves but it was more accident than skill that had her riding them. We laughed a lot and had fun. I didn't think about school or Merrin or Mel.

Amity drove me back to my house, our surfboards wedged between the seats of her sedan. She was so relaxed and sure of herself, driving along in a wetsuit with local radio blaring out of the speakers. I wondered if she'd ever been a Beach Rat, had ever slid her hand up some unsuspecting guy's leg while he perved on his Catholic Studies teacher.

'What are you doing tonight?' she asked.

'I dunno. Studying?' I didn't sound convincing, even to myself. 'There're a few parties. I dunno.'

I thought about the party Mel had mentioned. I didn't even know where it was on.

'Come round,' Amity said. 'Bring some notes and I'll quiz you. If you get the questions right you can have a beer. Shit — is that cop stopping here?' She eyed Dad pulling into the driveway beside her.

'Yeah — that's my Dad. You'd better not corrupt his youngest son.' I laughed as Amity swallowed hard and stared at me. 'See you later.' I wrestled my board out of the car as she waved politely at Dad who had stopped to water the front garden.

Amity was good to study with. She went over stuff with me and didn't seem to care if it took ten times for me to get it right. It was different to studying with Mel or Dan. I wasn't competing. I didn't have to rush my answers. After a couple of hours, Amity declared that my working week was finished. She gave me a beer and melted cheese on toast.

'Don't tell your dad.' She gestured to the beer and smiled.

'He's cool.' I bit into the toast but I could tell she was still thinking about Senior Sergeant Worthy.

'So,' she picked at the edge of her toast, as though

testing its quality. 'What's your favourite subject?'

'Catholic Studies.'

Amity raised her eyebrows.

'Hot teacher,' I explained.

She laughed. 'Worst?'

'Probably English.'

'Ugly teacher?'

I laughed. 'Nah — not too bad. It's just, you know, expressing yourself. All that "interpreting what the author wanted to say". They've said it already. It's written in the book. Why do I have to express my opinion about it? And who gives a toss what I think?'

Amity considered this. 'I loved English. I loved trying to work out the subtexts and the deeper meanings. I really liked poetry. Coleridge and all those.'

'Mel's the same. It's a girl thing. Dan goes alright in English, but Mel's fully into it, you know?'

'So who's Mel?'

And suddenly I was crapping on. Talking chick-shit. All about Mel and how she lived two doors away and how we'd grown up together.

'I didn't know you had a girlfriend, Jonah.'

'I don't. She's not.' I looked up, alarmed. 'Her mum has cancer.'

'So?'

I shifted the deckchair. Scratched at a mozzie bite. Two frigging beers and I was telling my life story.

'I think she's with Ferret anyway.'

'Oh.' Amity opened another beer. 'Okay.'

'She's not my girlfriend,' I insisted. I didn't want any chance I had with Amity to be wrecked by Mel, especially since Mel was spending all her time with Ferret.

'So, you're just friends.' Amity smiled knowingly over the top of her beer.

'Yeah, so what?'

'Nothing.'

'What?' I was no good at chick-shit.

'Well — just friends? It sounds like …' She let her words trail away.

'Like what?'

'Oh, Jonah, you know what "just friends" means.'

'What does it mean then?' Apparently I had a lot to learn.

Amity raised her eyebrows, pulled a funny face. 'You know, Jonah. Sex?'

'There's definitely no sex.' I tipped the dregs of my beer onto the grass. 'Trust me.'

Amity didn't argue. She let the summer night sink down around us. After a while, I spoke again.

'So, based on what you've said, "just friends" actually translates to bed buddies, right?'

She nodded.

'Well,' I paused. 'We're just friends, aren't we?'

She laughed and shook her head.

I stayed for three more beers. As I walked home, I felt pretty good. I'd studied a bit and I wasn't going to be hung-over. It wasn't a bad way to spend a night. I was still a virgin though.

On Sunday morning I went for a surf. I stopped off at the Caravan Park to pick up Ferret but his mum said she didn't know where he was. I did and was disgusted.

'Get down, you pervert.'

Ferret was flat on his stomach on the ladies' amenity block. He often climbed up there to perve on the women through the skylights.

He frowned at me and pressed a finger to his lips, showing me to keep quiet. He scrambled over the roof and dropped expertly onto the ground.

'Your girlfriend's in there right now. Rubbing tanning lotion all over her legs. She's so —'

'I don't want to know. Shut up. Shut up.' I covered my ears and tried not to think of Amity naked. Tried not to think of Ferret watching her be naked. 'Get your board and text Dan. I'll see you down there.'

'Okay. I'll call Mel too.' He jogged back towards his house.

I didn't wait for them on the beach, just went straight out. It was like the ocean was calling me: *Jonah, Jonah, Jonah*. I went in off the rocks and drifted, conserving energy rather than paddling through the break. The sets were reasonable and there weren't many people. I caught a few good waves before Ferret and Dan arrived. Some older guys out the back recognised me, asked if I was

Link's brother.

'He was a legend,' said one guy.

'Yeah — good bloke.'

'Nice to know ya.' They paddled away and I wondered if I was destined to live in Link's shadow.

The waves got bigger with the rising tide and I found myself thinking of Merrin. I had stupid thoughts too — like if I could catch the next wave, she would get better. If I could ride the next one through without coming off, the cancer would disappear. If I could pull off two turns ... if I could step along my board ... if I could catch three in a row ... I pushed myself harder and harder, trying to cure cancer in one good surf session. I stopped for a rest out the back, panting and frustrated. Dan and Ferret paddled in alongside me.

'You sick of living or something?'

'What?' I lay down on my board, let myself float.

'You were going mad. You're going to hurt yourself.'

'Nah.' I sat up again, watching the horizon. A cloud passed over the sun and the entire ocean seemed to turn grey. 'How was Friday night?'

'Awesome. You shoulda come, Joe. I was wasted, hey? Did nothing yesterday. Mel's still recovering. She was spewing everywhere.'

'Sounds good.' I angled my board around, hoping for an escape wave.

'And how was love fest?' Ferret turned to Dan.

'Got blisters on your pecker yet?'

'Not yet.' Dan was already paddling.

'Well, you're not trying hard enough!' Ferret shouted after him. He turned to talk to me, but I started paddling too. There wasn't a wave, but I just wanted to get away.

That night I reviewed my study timetable. I found the school newsletter and copied all the dates onto the calendar. Trials. Formals. Mum went through them with me and we counted off the weeks until the HSC would begin. Thirty. Thirty weeks. It sounded like a lifetime, but not quite long enough. I hung the calendar in my room and went out to the garage.

I got out all my boards and gave them a tune-up. I was thinking of letting Amity try my old thruster. She'd been using a big soft G-board, but I reckoned she could try a fibreglass. She had been better at surfing than I had anticipated, especially for a girl. Most of them were knackered just paddling out to the bar. Then again, she could've been one of those freaks — like Dan. The kind of person who excelled in everything they tried.

I repaired some hairline cracks and applied fresh coats of wax. I replaced a snapped leg rope and shook the sand out of my board bag. Then I got out Link's boards and gave them a hit. His newest one was hardly used so I left it out. It was a shame to have such a nice board just shoved in the shed. He'd never know.

Being a model now he might never surf again. I shook my head as I imagined him strutting down a catwalk. Modelling was a long way from surfing and I didn't really know how Link had arrived there. All that work to earn a place at uni and he'd chucked it in. Apparently life could take some unexpected turns once you got out of school. So was there any point in stressing about the future? Jobs and university and all that?

I lay in bed and sent Mel a text. Then I looked at the calendar and counted the weeks until school finished. Twenty-six. I opened the calendar to August and put a cross on my birthday. I had to have sex before then. I couldn't turn eighteen and still be a virgin. Part of me wished sex was a compulsory subject or like getting your Ps. Instead it was such a random thing, so simple but complex too. I needed it to be over so I could concentrate on other stuff. I fell asleep waiting for Mel's text but, even in the morning, she still hadn't replied.

6

Ferret had a car. It was a beat-up Datsun and it went like a piece of crap. He was revving it at the end of my driveway on Monday morning. Mum frowned at the sound, but Dad didn't even look up from the paper.

Mel was already in the front seat.

'What the ...?' I tumbled into the backseat, shoving empties out of the way.

'The time has come.' Ferret gripped the wheel before turning back to grin at me. 'I took out my entire life savings and had it insured, registered and all that crap. I was sick of seeing it parked there all lonely and sad.'

'But when did you?'

'When did I what?' Ferret revved again.

'Register it and all that?'

Mel turned to look at me, frowning. 'He's doing it this afternoon. Aren't you?' She looked pointedly at Ferret who shrugged.

'If you say so, babe.'

He put it into gear and took off, spluttering down the road and turning off towards Dan's place. Dan was equally surprised.

'But what about your olds?'

'They're away for a week. By the time they get back, it'll all be done. I'm nearly eighteen, damn it!' He turned a corner too quickly and the wheels screeched. I cheered and Dan, arm swinging out the open window, slapped his hand against the roof. Mel said nothing.

We arrived at school, feeling like legends as we pulled into the student car park. Most of the other seniors had cars — we were the last of the lot, but it still felt good. As we piled out, a group gathered. I heard someone ask Ferret if it was roadworthy and for the first time I noticed the massive rust patches over the wheels and around the bonnet.

'It could be a bloody tank and it wouldn't matter.' Ferret was boasting. 'I've got the long arm of the law on my side, hey, Jonah?'

I dragged out my bag and headed for class.

Ferret walked into English like he was the principal himself. He was carrying a briefcase and he slapped it down on the desk right next to me.

'Get lost.' I shoved his bag, but he grabbed it and sat down.

'I was just joking. You don't have to get snappy.'

'What've you got in there anyway?' I nudged the briefcase and watched him fiddle with the combinations. The teacher walked in then and we were reduced to whispers as she droned on about modern poets.

'I had a revelation — last Friday night. You want

in?' His voice was edgy.

'You said you were wasted. How could you have a revelation?'

'That's when the best ideas come, mate. I'm going into business.'

'What sort of business?'

The teacher frowned at me and I pretended to write notes.

'Can't tell ya.' Ferret never took his eyes from the front. When he wanted to, he could slip under the radar better than anyone. 'You in or not?'

'In what? What are you talking about?' I wrote something down on my page.

'Probably best not to.' He was patronising me now, pushing every button. 'You're too close to the law.'

'You're really pissing me off.'

'That's exactly what I mean.' He dropped the briefcase to the floor and took a pen from my pencil case.

Dan, Mel and I were watching Ferret from under the eucalypt. He was sauntering through the yard, stopping at the various groups and talking before moving along.

'What's he doing?'

'Who knows?' I stretched back on my bag and thought of Amanda Wellings. She probably wasn't as ugly as I thought.

Eventually Ferret made his way over to us.

'What are you up to?' Dan threw a tennis ball hard at him. Ferret used his briefcase as a shield.

'I'm networking.' He snapped open the case and pulled out his lunch.

'What?' Dan had the ball again and was practising his overarm bowling. In slow motion he went through the moves, without releasing the ball. Ferret ignored him and Dan did a bowl in full speed, stopping just short of Ferret's head. Ferret flinched and swore.

'You're a bully.' Ferret was serious. 'You can't let any of us have a little bit of space can you? You have to have it all.'

'Yeah, well, I just want to keep our space safe. You know? Clean.'

The bell went then, and Ferret snatched up his briefcase and walked away. I looked at Dan and then at Mel. She opened her hands and shrugged.

We rode home together in Ferret's car. Stacey came too, gripping onto Dan like some kind of suckerfish. I was glad I was in the front. Ferret was crapping on as usual, complaining about Mr Johnston and speculating about Jumper Girl. Even Mel was talkative. She told a funny story about something that happened in her extension English class.

Anyone would think we were one big happy family, crammed into the Dato like people who were actually close. But it was as though tectonic plates were shifting. I was annoyed with Ferret, he was angry at Dan, Mel was avoiding me. I glanced back at Stacey and wondered if she realised the dynamics had changed. Dan was drawing a little tattoo on her shoulder. She was squirming and giggling. Mel was pressed up against the car door so I moved my seat forward.

'Have you got enough room there, Mel?'

'Yeah. I just hope I don't catch an STI with all this freakin' love here in the back.'

'Hey!' Ferret tooted the horn. 'No sex in the back. Not while I'm driving. It's not insured.'

We all laughed and Ferret tooted again. Maybe things were okay. I didn't know anymore.

7

I wasn't sure I could survive Year 12. The first few weeks nearly killed me. Teachers were continually testing us, ranking us, reviewing our work, picking holes in our efforts. Generally making us feel hopeless. The work just kept piling up and my HSC countdown calendar was already covered with test times and due dates. I couldn't tell what was important anymore. A math quiz worth fifteen per cent or an English essay worth twenty?

Term 1 dragged along. Dan seemed to cruise through things, breaking up his study and stress by using Stacey for some light relief. I felt jealous and once I even got a hard-on watching them pash on the playground in the shade of the tree.

Normally Ferret would've been around to inject a bit of humour but it was like he was missing in action these days. He had a string of people coming in and out of our area and he was always encouraging them to sit round with us. Dan was sick of it. We'd always been The Surfers and he didn't like The Plastics, The Spastics, The Squares, The Gangsters, The Jocks or The Try-Hards encroaching on our space. He didn't really like The Rats either but he tolerated them because of the fringe benefits.

Things were changing. I couldn't remember the last time we'd all surfed together and Amanda Wellings was ringing me every other night. But even though everything was different, life had become a treadmill. It was school and study, school and study, school and study.

And when I wasn't studying, I couldn't seem to get my act together. I knew I should talk to Mel and visit Merrin. I needed a good surf. But I just bummed around, killing time until there was a party and then I'd get trashed.

Before Year 12, partying was something extra. It wasn't a priority — not like surfing. But now, it was intense. We were desperate to get out of our lives, to get out of ourselves. Most weekends I'd get wasted. Drunk and disorderly was the way to go. And I wasn't alone.

Ferret was the heart and soul of every night out. He was calling himself the Ripper Stripper and he'd turn up to parties wearing his wetsuit, flippers and snorkel. By the end of the night he'd be down to just the snorkel and he could do some pretty bizarre stuff with it, all of it unhygienic. I started to think that Ripper Stripper was the great business idea he'd been crapping on about but I couldn't work out how a naked Ferret would generate any income.

I stripped off with him one night. After drinking too much bourbon it seemed like the logical thing to do. I free-balled my way up and down Amanda

Wellings' hallway while everyone cheered me on. It ended badly though, with Amanda hiding my clothes and making a dangerous grab for my balls as I staggered from her house.

By the end of Term 1, things were getting messy. I was going out every Friday and Saturday night. I was wasting money, avoiding study and Mum was pissed off. I think I was out of control. It's hard to know what you are when you're spewing up bourbon on the front lawn.

Amity found me on the last Saturday of the Term 1 holidays. I was beyond trashed and had fallen asleep outside the pub. We'd been at a party, just me, Dan and Ferret. Mel never went out these days. Dan had stayed at the party with Stacey. They looked as though they might have been going to break a world record for dry humping. Ferret had come with me to the pub, he needed my Canberra Clothes and 'older' good looks to help him get in the door, but when Amity woke me he was nowhere to be seen.

She led me away from the pub and we went in a taxi to her van. She made me drink coffee and cold water. I think I even passed out on her bed. At some stage I woke up and she was beside me.

'What are you doing, Jonah?'

'Sleeping with you?' I raised my eyebrows hopefully, but she didn't laugh.

'You were absolutely out of your tree. Look at yourself.'

I sat up slowly and saw that my pants were wet. I lay back down and rubbed my hands over my face. The van was spinning and I wished she'd stop talking.

'And Ferret? What's he been taking? He's an idiot.'

'Ah, Ferret's alright. He's my friend.' I sat up and vomited all over her.

I stayed until morning, letting the night pass in waves of nausea and unconsciousness. As the early morning light found its heat, I scraped myself up and tried to thank Amity for looking after me. I was rewarded with a lecture.

'What do you prove by drinking like that?'

I rubbed my head and tried to let my double vision merge. She had her arms folded and her tits were pressed together. It was a lovely double-vision image.

'Think of next year. That's when you can drink your life away. Next year.'

I groaned and let my body roll back onto the bed.

'That's the problem.' I mumbled it into the pillow, hoping she'd stop tricking me into another psychoanalysis of myself.

'What problem?'

'Next year.'

'Why? What's your plan?'

I groaned again, felt sickness swell inside me and then fall away.

'My plan is ...' I waited. 'My plan is finish school,

go to schoolies, hang around for a year, go back to schoolies as a toolie. Then get a gig on a reality TV show.' I sat up and noticed one shoe was gone.

'That's it? That's your plan?'

'It's a crap plan. I know. Where's my shoe?'

'You only had one.' Amity shook her head and sat beside me. 'There's lots you could do, Jonah.'

I could feel the school counsellor-slash-motivational speaker brewing inside her, so I stood up. The van seemed to sway dangerously and I leant on the tiny kitchen table.

'I know, I know. I've got lots to offer, a bright future. I can't cure cancer though, can I?'

Amity looked up at me. She didn't seem golden any more. She had a dark red birthmark on one side of her neck and her teeth were crooked. She was still beautiful, but she was just a person. She stared at me and I realised I was beyond embarrassment. She'd seen my best and my worst. And she wasn't going to sleep with me, either way.

'You need to talk to Mel.' She nodded, as though she'd just worked out some tricky algebraic equation. 'I know what this is all about. You've got to sort yourself out mate, or you'll leave school with more baggage than a forty-year-old divorcee.'

'You're crapping on.' I limped towards the door, wondering why every part of my body was aching.

'Talk to Mel.' Her voice was firm. 'Today.'

I staggered out the caravan door and was startled by the sun.

8

'Don't talk to me. Don't even look at me.' They were Mum's first words as I arrived home. She snatched at the phone and pressed speed dial. 'He's here. He's home.' She paused, listening. 'I didn't ask. I don't care.' She hung up and then stalked outside.

I limped into my room, still wearing only one shoe. Piles of books stood to attention, ready to be studied and learnt. I flopped onto my bed and slept. When I woke, the books were still there. Unstudied. Unlearnt. I kicked one pile over, watching the way they fell at angles, balancing with all their wisdom still enclosed.

I threw off my clothes and tugged on my boardies. I stopped at Mel's and was surprised when she agreed to come with me. We walked all the way to Bar, but it was flat.

'Short Point?' Mel suggested.

'Yep.'

We trudged along together, falling into step and keeping our eyes to the ground. We didn't talk. My head was still aching and the board felt heavier with every step. Drinking was overrated.

I went straight in, burrowing under the waves and

letting the salty water enclose me. The waves were small but powerful and I rode four of them in a row. My mind went blank as I negotiated each one, letting the hum of the ocean consume me. I went further out the back as a few larger sets came in. I worked with the energy of each wave, testing my mettle against its own. I came off a few, slapped down like a piece of crap.

On the sand, I sat next to Mel. My head was still throbbing and I was starving.

'Are we fighting?' I looked at her and then turned away, drew a little picture in the sand.

'I don't know. No.' She sighed as she spoke and it was like a door was opening, just a tiny bit. 'I just don't have time for any of the usual crap, you know what I mean? It's like I've got Year 12 and Mum and then you and Ferret. I just can't.' She shifted her foot, digging into the sand so it disappeared.

'Yeah, Amity reckons —'

'I don't want to hear about her.' She snapped the words out at me without looking up.

I paused and wondered what was going on. I crafted a little sandcastle and decorated it with a cigarette butt. Mel kicked it and smiled at me. I grabbed her foot and she laughed. We wrestled for a moment, letting laughter fill the space between us. Then we fell back on the sand, watching perfect white clouds shift across the sky.

'Seriously though.' I waited, wondering if we were really alright. 'Are you and Ferret together?'

She sat up and turned to me. She rolled her eyes and let out a disbelieving little grunt.

'You don't get it, do you? You just ...' She sighed and shook her head.

'Mel, I just want to know.'

'You're like all the others.' She stood up and dusted the sand from her bum. 'Talk to Ferret. Ask him. And while you're there, ask about the drugs.'

She marched away, her feet punching into the dry sand like angry little fists. I jogged after her but she kept a step ahead of me the whole way home.

That night I still felt awful. Everything seemed to be magnified into dynamic proportions. I could still see Mel's feet stomping away from me over the sand. I thought about what she had said, about Ferret and the drugs. I'd obviously missed something there. Was he into the hardcore stuff? Dealing it? Out of a bloody briefcase? Dickhead.

So maybe Ferret and Mel weren't together. Maybe she was just counselling him through his latest stuff-up. I didn't know shit anymore.

Dad gave me a roasting when he got home from the cop shop. His main point seemed to be the near-death experience Mum had suffered as a result of my absence. As usual, his supporting arguments went along the lines of me needing to be a model citizen since he was a senior sergeant. I'd heard that speech so many times I couldn't even be bothered arguing.

Then Link rang.

'What the hell's going on down there?'

'Nothing.' I still hadn't eaten and it didn't seem that Mum was going to cook anything for dinner. I was meant to suffer.

'Mum rings me this morning wanting to know where you are. Then she rings me this afternoon wanting to know when I'm coming home. She's on edge.'

'Yeah I know.' I rubbed at my head and tried to feel concerned.

'It could be menopause, you know.'

'What?'

'You know, the change of life when a woman stops getting her periods.'

'Well, she should be happy. Girls spend their entire lives whinging about it and when it goes away they become monsters.' At that moment Mum walked past my room looking like a guerrilla terrorist. I stretched out my leg and kicked the door closed.

'I'd better come down,' Link said. 'It's time.'

'Time for what?'

'Time to tell them.'

'Good idea.' It hadn't been hard keeping Link's modelling a secret, but things would be easier if I didn't have to get nervous every time Target dropped a catalogue in our letterbox.

'No time like the present.' Link drawled it out in a funny accent.

'Yeah.'

'So I'll start right now.'

'What are you on about?'

'I'm bringing my friend down.'

'Okay.'

'My friend Sam?'

I paused, recalled the girls I had met in Canberra. Kat, Lucy, Tilly, Veronica. No Sam.

'Remember?' Link insisted. 'You met Sam. The day before you left.'

A hazy memory faded in. Sam had arrived while we were doing weights. Tall and lean. Dark hair, dark eyes. A good-looking guy really.

'Sam the guy? When you said friend I thought you meant *friend* — you know, girlfriend.'

'I do mean *friend*.'

I listened to the hush of the line as I waited for Link to crack up laughing.

'Feet?'

'My name's Jonah.'

'Okay, Jonah. Don't tell Mum. Let me tell her, in my own way.'

I nodded, forgetting he couldn't see me.

'Jonah?'

'Yeah, yeah, whatever.' My mind tried to race ahead and process what he was saying.

'Are you okay? I'm still Link you know. Still your big brother.'

'Yeah, I know.'

There was another pause and a late wave of nausea rose within, reminding me how bad everything seemed right now.

'So don't tell Mum?' he insisted.

'Yeah, right,' I shook my head, trying to focus. 'What about Dad?'

'He's cool.' Link's tone was light and I wondered how he could be so sure that Senior Sergeant Worthy wasn't going to arrest him for providing misleading information or breach of trust or something.

'Dad's cool with this?' I wanted to be sure.

'Yeah. Don't worry about him. Where were you last night anyway? Mum was freaking out this morning.'

'I stayed at Amity's caravan.'

'Bull.'

'I did.' I laughed then, realising that Link was going to be in bigger trouble than I'd ever known. 'And it doesn't matter anyway 'cause the spotlight's on you now.'

'Hey, keep your voice down. Just sit tight till I get there, okay? And go easy on Sam. This'll be difficult for him too.'

I hung up the phone and wondered who it was I'd just been talking to.

According to some, I was the new local legend when it came to pulling chicks. A few of the lads had seen Amity collect me from the pub and her gorgeous looks hadn't gone unnoticed.

'Even wasted you can reel 'em in,' Lewis Frescombe shouted to me as I walked through the school gates. He thrust his pelvis around and I wondered how Amity would react if she could see him.

'Nice work,' said another guy as I walked into roll call. He even patted me on the back as though I'd won some kind of competition. And just like the Lindsay inter-school sports saga, I didn't bother to stop and correct them. Word must've gotten around to Dan.

'So you're shagging that Siren after all?' He was walking next to me into Catholic Studies. 'You should take the sex-box lessons. You'd know more than Finlay.'

'So would you.'

Dan shrugged, dropped his bag onto a desk and said quietly, 'Stacey's a lot of things but she's no Siren, mate. Enjoy it.'

I wanted to feel proud, but I knew it was all lies. I thought of Link and wondered if that whole conversation had been for real. Was he really gay? Or was he just yanking my chain? I remembered that day in the mall, all that homo PC stuff. He'd lied to me.

Then Mel came in and gave me a look that was worse than my mother's face on Sunday morning. She was pissed off. I didn't think things were that bad. I let my head rest on my desk and felt a final wave of nausea as I leant forward. Saturday night was still haunting me.

'Good work, Jonah.' Ferret slapped me on the back as he walked past. There was no teacher in the room, so he leapt onto the desk and put on a quick show. He swung his hips back and forth. Then he let out a high-pitched wail and said, 'The Siren's coming.' He froze in position as he swivelled round and saw Ms Finlay framed in the doorway. Then he said something I'll never forget. 'You want some of this, babe?' He shifted his hips forward and looked straight at her.

'Out.' Ms Finlay wasn't joking around.

Ferret's show had at least taken the focus off me. He was suspended for three days and didn't seem to give a toss. Dan and I met up with him each afternoon supposedly to review the day's lessons, but we ended up surfing every time.

It felt good. Ferret was more daring than ever, managing to pull off some awesome tricks on his boogie board. Dan was aiming for precision, surfing each wave as though it was a science.

'If that'd been the HSC, I'd have got a hundred per cent,' he said as we waited for the next set.

I took Link's newest board down and carved up the waves without any kind of plan. It just felt good to be back in the salt with Dan and Ferret. I didn't think about Mel or Amity or Link and Sam. And we didn't talk study or suspension or Stacey. We were three islands in the same ocean.

It was the day before Ferret was due back at school that Dan asked about the drugs.

'Are you taking shit?' We were on the hill at Short looking down at the water.

'I'm always taking shit.' Ferret was quick. 'Mainly from you, Danny Boy.'

'Don't call me that.'

I stood up, trying to distance myself. I'd never faced up to Dan like Ferret was. I didn't know whether to feel scared or envious.

'Yeah, I'm taking stuff,' Ferret admitted. 'Everyone does. You're taking Stacey, Jonah's on the grog, I'm on the Dex. What's your point?'

'No point,' Dan said, suddenly patronising. 'No point at all really, is there, Ferret?'

'Screw you.'

'No, screw you, Ferret.'

'Hey, guys.' They looked up at me and I wondered what I was meant to say. 'Settle.'

Ferret laughed, stood up and then dropped onto Dan, wrestling him playfully. Dan attacked, letting a hint of aggression pulse through him before he let go of Ferret who lay laughing and defeated on the grass.

'Whenever you're ready guys,' Ferret said. 'I'll give you a taste.' He was still laughing when Dan's mobile rang and Stacey's voice came trilling out of the phone.

I was trying to discreetly return Link's board into its bag when Dad found me in the garage.

'What are you doing?' he asked.

'Nothing.' I shoved the board into the bag and tried to zip my guilt away with it. I pulled out another board and rested it on the workbench, pretending to check it over.

'I know what's going on,' Dad said, idly tugging at the leg rope.

I kept my eyes trained on the board and ran through every possibility he might be talking about. The unregistered Dato? My nights at the pub? Drinking under age? Ferret and the Dex? I let the silence fill up the garage. I didn't want to confess to the wrong thing.

'About Link,' Dad said and I almost swore. More possibilities: the modelling, uni drop out, the gay thing. I couldn't believe I had so many secrets and Dad knew one of them — maybe more. I decided to incriminate myself, just a little bit. I'd throw a line out and see what the bait brought in.

'Yeah, I used his board.' I nodded towards the bag leaning against the wall. 'His new one.'

'No, Feet.' Dad put his hand on my shoulder. 'I know about Link. Know he's gay.'

'Oh, that.' I laughed nervously, still looking down at the board, noticing the tiny lumps and grooves that somehow helped to hold me steady when I rode it.

'It's okay, mate,' Dad squeezed my shoulder. 'It'll be okay.'

'You reckon?' I risked a look at him, letting every one of my fears meet him face-to-face.

'Yeah, I reckon.' Dad leant back against the workbench and folded his arms across his chest. 'As long as he's happy. I just want you boys to be happy.' He sighed and something like defeat flickered across his face.

I considered what he'd said. Happiness. I didn't know that was a priority for Senior Sergeant Worthy.

I thought about how the gay news might go down at the station. Would Dad get hassled when the other cops got hold of the news? Was the cop shop PC? Or was it more like school? Dog-eat-dog until there was only one man standing.

'Don't you think it's weird?' I ran my hands over the board before glancing again at Dad.

It was resignation I could see on his face: beyond defeat and closer to acceptance.

'Yeah, it's weird,' he agreed. 'And I didn't see it coming. But it could be worse, I guess.' He sighed again.

'Worse?'

'Feet, there are far worse things.' He unfolded his arms. 'Link could be stealing cars or abusing women. He could be on drugs or putting other people in danger.' He paused and I suddenly felt guilty again.

I thought about Ferret and the drugs, my recent drinking sprees and that stupid unregistered Datsun. Surely being gay was worse than all that. I was the good son, the straight son. Hell — I was the virgin.

'But Dad, he's gay,' I insisted. 'For real. He's gay. A poofter, you know? A fag.'

He nodded, shifted his body away from the

workbench. 'Yep. I know. But he's happy.'

I watched Dad walk out of the garage and saw him shrug, as though he was talking to himself. And I could tell then that he was just like me. Still trying to make sense of it all.

Mum was excited about Link's visit. She even came to my room and asked if I'd met Sam.

'What's she like?' Mum's eyes were bright, Link had never brought a friend home from uni before.

'Not what you'd expect.' I kept my eyes down, trying to focus on my essay.

'Do you think they're ...' Mum let her voice trail off.

'What? Do I think they're what?' I turned to Mum, letting my frustration show. This was typical Link, overshadowing my days with secrets and crap.

'Are they, you know? Together?'

'Dunno.' I turned back to my work and she eventually left my room. Poor Mum. She didn't know what was coming her way.

I wandered up the road to Mel's, telling myself I needed help with my essay. The truth was I just needed help. I had to make things right with Mel; I hated it when she was angry. I wanted to tell her about Link.

But Mel wasn't home and her dad answered the door. Geoff looked tired and his eyes were dull. It was an instant reality check. Merrin had cancer. She could die.

'Feet. Good to see you.' Geoff shook my hand and slapped my shoulder. Then he pulled me in and hugged me. I patted his back and felt like a bastard.

'Mel here?'

'No, no. She's at Ferret's or somewhere studying. No, actually,' he rubbed his face and frowned, 'she's at school. One of the teachers was running a study afternoon, so she stayed back for it. That's right. Listen, I don't suppose you could stay here for a bit? Merrin's really tired and I need to get to the shops.'

'No worries,' I lied, hoping I didn't have to stay for long.

'Oh, great.' He was out the door before I knew it and I couldn't blame him.

Merrin was in the lounge room. Even her clothes looked sick. She was crumpled and stale. There were tissues and drink bottles and medicines dotted along the coffee table. I gave her a kiss and she smelt like the hospital.

'Hello, Jonah,' she said warmly, reaching for the remote and turning the volume down. 'Mel's not here.'

'I know. I saw Geoff. He's just run to the shops.'

'God love him.' She looked at me and I could see the animal in her eyes, helpless and trapped. I sat next to her on the lounge and tried not to stare at the patchy hair standing in tufts from her head. She must've started treatment and I hadn't even known.

'Tell me news, all news,' her words were jumbled and slurred. She burped and was too slow to cover her mouth. I smiled and launched into a long spiel, wanting to tell her anything to take her away from the suffering.

She smiled and laughed as I told her about Link. I went through the whole thing, from the uni dropout to the modelling, finishing with the gay bombshell and his impending visit with Sam.

'But Mum doesn't know. So don't say anything, or Link'll eat my balls for breakfast.'

Merrin laughed. 'Your poor Mum.'

'Yeah.' I sighed. 'She thinks Sam's a girl.'

Merrin laughed again, a long laugh that momentarily lit her up. Her spark was still there and it made me feel good. Mel walked in, just as I was helping Merrin press her tablets out of their oversized plastic bubble.

'I'll do that.' Mel stepped past me and arranged things.

'I was just going anyway.' I turned to the door and dropped my essay on a nearby chair. 'Could you look at that for me?'

Mel nodded, then turned back to her mum.

'See you later, Feet.' Merrin smiled at me and I winked, putting a finger to my lips showing our little secret. She laughed again and I left feeling okay, even if Mel was still angry.

Link arrived on Friday night. I opened the door and he handed me a large cylinder.

'It's Pamela. She was missing you.' I pulled out the

shiny poster and stared at Pam. She was still smiling and her tits looked fabulous. I almost felt like kissing them.

Sam stood behind Link, waiting patiently. He was wearing a collared shirt and a tie. If he'd been wearing a jacket he'd have looked ready to accept an Academy Award.

Mum bounded down the stairs, singing something about wanting to see her handsome boy. She froze as she spotted Sam, standing like a bodyguard behind Link. Link stepped back, positioning himself next to Sam and sliding his arm around him in a way that meant things were serious.

'Mum,' Link's voice didn't even falter, 'I'd like you to meet my good friend, Sam.'

9

In the end, it was Mum who deserved the Academy Award. She did the best acting of her life that night, standing in our front doorway with a big fake smile plastered on her face. She welcomed Sam and closed the door, noticing Link's arm still curled around Sam's back. Behind them, she glared at me. I shrugged, showing I had no insider knowledge. I didn't really, just twenty-four hours' notice.

I understood where Mum was coming from. It was weird. It seemed wrong watching the way Link moved around Sam. But, there was a gentleness there and a truth. As though I'd known something all along but was only just realising it.

Mum bustled around the kitchen, cooking and setting the table. She asked how their drive had been and told them about the weather. And more than once she wondered aloud how late our father was going to be. Mum was a closed book. For now.

Full credit to Link though, he went about things as though nothing had changed. He shadow-boxed with me and asked about Merrin. He looked at my study timetable and quizzed me on my teachers. Link opened a bottle of wine and poured Mum a large glass.

But the entire time he had one eye on Sam. When Mum commented again how late Dad was, Link showed Sam to the spare room.

While he was gone Mum skulled her glass of wine and poured another. She watched me watching her and squinted an interrogating look at me. I held my hands up in surrender and she sipped her wine thoughtfully. Then she poured one for me too.

Sam emerged from the spare room and immediately complimented Mum on what a nice house she had. He looked at the black-and-white photos artfully arranged on the lounge-room walls and asked if they were local scenes. Mum weakened momentarily and explained her passion for photography. Sam listened attentively and asked about the type of cameras she preferred. And as she answered, Mum poured him a generous glass of red.

Dad finally arrived home and didn't even bat an eyelid when Link ran through his good friend routine. In fact, Dad turned his attention to me and explained that he was late because he'd been chasing hoons in an unregistered vehicle. I frowned at him and shrugged.

'Well, that sucks,' I offered, trying to work out how it was my problem.

'Yeah — *sucks* is a word for it.' Dad was in full officer mode. '*Illegal* would be another one. Or even *difficult position*.' He looked at me pointedly and I finally clicked that Ferret was the hoon. He hadn't bothered to register the Dato.

Dad turned to Sam and switched on his friendly parent persona. He apologised again for being late and asked Sam what he did for a living and how he'd met Link.

Over dinner, Mum kept the wine coming. By 10 p.m. I'd had four full glasses of red. I could've had more but I was sick of the politically correct conversation. As I pushed my chair away from the table, I told Sam it had been nice meeting him again. Link smiled up at me and actually mouthed the words *thank you* while no one else could see.

He was gayer than I thought.

The next morning Link dragged me out of bed and made me run the bike path from Merimbula to Pambula. It felt good to be working hard at something and to have company while I was doing it. More than one girl gave us a wave as we went by and I tried to imagine how that made Link feel. Powerful or guilty? Like he was deceiving everyone?

We walked home slowly with Link talking the entire time. He said that being gay was the way he was born. Apparently I couldn't catch it. And he told me there was no such thing as a poofter radar; a 'gaydar'. The thing was, I still didn't think of Link as being gay. He was just Link, my brother.

Back home, he dragged a bucket of protein powder

out of his bag and insisted that we do weights that afternoon.

'We don't have any,' I said.

'I brought mine. Sam got me a new set so you can have my old gear. We'll set it up out the back.'

'Nah, let's go for a surf this arv. It's been good at Short.'

'Yeah,' Link persisted, 'after we've done the weights.'

'Slave driver.'

'Lazy boy.'

'Fag.'

'Jonah, don't. It's not —'

'PC. Yeah, I know.' I tipped the last of the shake down the sink and headed out of the kitchen.

'Joe.'

'What?' I turned around expecting another lecture on how I should speak to the newly self-proclaimed gay relative.

'Take Sam out for me this morning? Show him 'round? I need time with Mum.'

I rolled my eyes, knowing that I would've looked exactly like Stacey. But just as I was going to tell him to get stuffed I had a sudden vision of Merrin and then of Mum. It was time I did something decent.

'Alright.' I looked up at him and decided to start laying down some terms of my own. 'But I'm not talking PC and I'm not going shopping with him. I had enough of that with you in Canberra, ya Nancy.'

Link smiled at me then. 'Thanks, Feet. I owe you.'

I took Sam to the beach. I didn't tell Dan or Ferret. I didn't even call Mel. I wasn't sure how I felt about hanging out with a gay guy.

I wasn't even sure how gay Sam was. He wasn't 'gay-gay'. At first I had panicked thinking he might be like one of those fags off the Mardi Gras floats. I didn't want to have to go around town with some transvestite dressed in hot-pink feathers. But he didn't dress gay and he didn't talk gay either. His voice was normal and he wore typical Canberra Clothes. He was built like an athlete, an iron man really. He had a sharp chiselled face, like the guys on razor ads. He looked like a normal guy — someone that Stacey would stick her tits out for.

I wondered again how gay guys felt when chicks flirted with them. Did gays even notice things on women, like good legs and nice tits? They probably thought about long dicks and hairy bums. I remembered the black guy in the poster. My brain ran into overdrive.

'It's a beautiful place here,' Sam was saying.

I nodded, trying to kill off the gay porn that was germinating in my mind.

'Just park anywhere.' I had brought him to Main Beach. There was no surf and less chance of running into anyone from school.

I led the way onto the sand, trying to keep a step

ahead, just in case the 'gaydar' thing was true. We dumped our towels and Sam headed straight for the water. I chose to lie on my towel and I tried to remember the last time I'd done that. Towel lying was a Beach Rat sport, but I couldn't bring myself to go into the water with Sam. I even moved his towel over so it wasn't touching mine. Born gay, my arse: it could be as contagious as the flu and science just hadn't realised yet.

A pack of farmers were arriving on the beach. I thought of Ferret making jokes about their footy shorts and the singlet-shaped sunburn crisped onto their skin. Their chests were as white as the sheep they'd left behind and they called out to one another with nicknames like Wombat, Red and Codger. They dropped their tiny motel towels near ours and started kicking the footy in among the shallows.

'Wee Wah boys with wee willies,' Ferret would've said. They were probably good lads, but we'd always hated country punters, especially when they tried to surf. These guys seemed harmless enough, until Red booted the footy out deep and it landed near Sam.

Of course Sam was all over it, retrieving the footy and emerging from the waves with the equivalent in male sexiness that Amity had oozed that first time I saw her. He was a male Bond girl. He jogged up to the lads and I felt myself cringing. *Just kick it back to them you Nancy. Don't go fagging all over them.* I tried to send him my thoughts, but he just continued towards them. *There's going to be a gay-bashing*, I thought. *Right here on Main Beach*.

'Thanks, mate.' Wombat nodded as Sam finally palmed the ball off to him. Sam smiled and they started talking.

I stood up, holding my towel and took a step away from where Sam's towel was lying in a crumpled heap. I didn't want to become gay by association.

I watched them talk for a moment. Two other blokes moved in closer and idly bounced the footy. Eventually Sam found his way back to his towel leaving the Wee Wah boys kicking the football. He dried off while I watched the farmers carefully, waiting for them to detect Sam's gayness and come after him. They didn't though. They either couldn't tell or didn't care. I wondered if there were many poofters in Wee Wah.

'You should go in, Jonah. It's beautiful.' Sam slumped onto the sand with his towel strapped tight around his hips. That was how Dan always wrapped his towel after a surf. Was Dan a homo too? My entire brain gayed out.

I dropped my towel and ran into the surf. I threw myself under the waves and swam out the back, dodging kids on boogie boards and old men in Speedos. *Link's gay*. I dived down and clenched my fists into the sand, pulling myself against the force of the wave. *Link's gay with Sam*. Down again, dragging against the suction. *Link and Sam kiss*. Down again, resisting, fighting against the inevitable. *And they have sex*. I let the wave hit me. Full force.

But it didn't knock me down. I was still standing.

Amanda Wellings had seen me at Main. She sent me a text that afternoon while I was assembling the weights with Link.

Who is ur cute friend?

He is gay. I replied and immediately regretted it. Her response arrived quickly.

I could fix that. LOL.

I showed Link her messages and he raised his eyebrows and smiled.

'Yeah, people say that,' he said and continued setting up the weights bench.

'I don't get it,' I huffed, lugging a stack of weights in from his car. 'Could a chick really fix you?'

Link sighed and sat on the bench, testing his workmanship. The crack in the vinyl had grown and more stuffing was oozing out.

'It's like I told Mum,' he explained patiently. 'I'm still Link. It's just now I'm myself. I'm gay. I always have been. It's not anything you've done or I've done or Mum or Dad did. It's just what I am. It's what makes me happy.'

'I'd be happy shagging double-Ds every night, but I can't go around and do it though.'

Link shook his head. 'It's not a sex thing, Feet. Well it is, but it's more than that. I'm not just indulging in a fantasy. Do you know what I mean?'

I thought of Amity and of Amanda. Blood lust and potential blood lust.

'Nuh,' I said finally. 'I don't get it and I never will. And you'll go off to Canberra and live your pooncey little life and I'll be here getting slagged on because my big brother's a poofter. And before you start all that PC crap, let me tell you that's what people will say. That's what we say around here. Homo and poofter. And now it's like I'm in amongst all of that.' I dropped a pile of weights letting them fall dangerously close to his feet.

'Well you've got a lot of baggage to deal with, haven't you?' Link wasn't happy. 'What's really on your mind? Why don't you stop all this homophobic crap and just tell me what your problem is? Because I thought we were friends. Brothers and friends. I thought you'd be okay with this.' He kicked at the weights and stood up.

'I am okay with it.' I sat on the bench and picked at the stuffing, remembering the waves. He screws blokes. I can't change that. 'I just wish ...' I let my voice trail off, glancing up at the house to check Mum wasn't on the deck listening.

'What?' Link scratched his neck, wiped a hand over his face. He looked tired and kind of sad.

'I just wish you could've waited until I'd had a root. You know, confirmed my own sexual ...' I paused. 'You know, my own, sexual compass.'

Link laughed hard, the sound echoing off the garage walls. 'Compass?' He tried to keep his face steady.

'Oh, shut up.' I loaded the bar onto the support

and started securing the weights.

We trained hard, adjusting equipment and shifting things between sets. Every now and then Link would start laughing and I'd give him the finger.

'I'm happy now, Feet.' Link said as we wiped down the gear at the end of the session. 'I wasn't before, but now I am. And if Mum asks you about it, tell her that I'm happy, okay?'

I nodded, sensing how serious things must have been at home while I was enduring my gay nightmare at Main Beach.

'And I'm sorry about your sexual compass, but I couldn't wait for your first root until I came out.' He tried not to smile. 'I couldn't wait till I was forty!'

Link was still laughing when I walked out.

We didn't surf that afternoon. Link took Sam for a drive and did whatever it was that gay guys did. I tried to study but I couldn't get into it. I sent a text to Amity and then one to Mel. No reply. Out of sheer desperation I sent one to Amanda. She replied straight away and we messaged back and forth for about an hour. In the end she wanted to meet me down the street. But I just wanted a distraction, not a whole big commitment thing, so I stopped replying.

I unrolled Pamela and pinned her on the wall at the end of my bed. I lay there and looked up at her, imagining all kinds of good clean heterosexual things we could do together. I was pleased to see Pam again and just when I thought I might've taken things a bit further, I heard a car in the driveway. Then Link and Sam's voices and laughter. And then, the unmistakable pause, where a kiss might fit, right outside my window. My dick curled away in horror.

That night Link came into my room and woke me up.

'Get lost,' I managed to bleat.

'Come on. Get dressed and get your board. Meet you outside.'

We hadn't night-surfed in years. As I threw on boardies and searched for a towel, I tried to remember the last time we'd done it. It was the best kind of surfing: freaking out in the darkness and paranoid that Dad would find out. It gave every ride an edge.

We walked in silence to Short, our wetsuits slung over our shoulders like empty dead bodies. Link had his new board and I had my little 5'9" single fin. I wondered if I should've brought something more familiar, broader and bigger, but we were halfway there and I didn't want to sound like a chicken.

The ocean was roaring as we jogged down the hill. It always sounded louder at night. I felt the panic start to seep in and looked at Link. His teeth flashed white in the darkness as he smiled.

'Are you bleaching your teeth now? You're worse than the chicks.'

He cuffed me over the head and we stripped off, wrestling ourselves into wetsuits that suddenly seemed to have minds of their own.

The water was cool on my face but barely touching my skin through the insulation of the suit. I thought of condoms and sex and wondered if a wetsuit was a similar sensation. An icy blade of water slipped into a pocket of air behind my neck and sliced down my spine. All thoughts of sex were abandoned as I pressed down beneath the first wave.

Link was ahead of me, settling on his board out the back. The moon cast a pale light on the expanse of ocean around him. He was in the spotlight.

A fresh set idled in, but Link waited until I had joined him. I felt the waves crest beneath me as I looked around, trying to gain my bearings in the night. The ocean rested again, lying still before her next deep breath.

'It's not everything, mate,' Link said, still looking out to sea. 'Sex isn't a big deal. Don't stress about it, okay?'

'I'm not,' I kept my face to the shore, wishing he hadn't said anything.

'Good.' He splashed in the water, patting his palm against the ripple. ''Cause Year 12's not the time to get hung up on stuff. You get one go at it and that's it.'

'Yeah, yeah, yeah.' I swivelled my board around and looked at the new set approaching. It was like watching opportunity arrive. Link smiled again, another fluorescent light bulb.

'I just want to know ...' I let my voice trail off,

lay down and waited for the wave.

'What?' Link turned, ready for shore.

'How would I know I'm doing it right? You know, sex?'

'You don't know.' Link was confident. 'I still don't know. It's like surfing. You just do what feels right.'

And then he was flying, letting the wave collect him and take him. He went with it, rising and falling along the face in a series of stylish moves, finishing with a mellow ride almost onto the sand. It was like he'd never been away from it.

Even gay, he was still a better surfer than me. I caught the next one and felt the grip of fear as I realised I was surfing blind. I heaved myself up and the wave looked black beneath me. I struggled to find my balance as I was shafted down the slippery face. At the last moment I turned, barely escaping the whitewater. I carved again and again, drawing further away from Link, eventually letting the wave melt beneath me.

I stayed out to the side, surfing apart from Link until I was enjoying the sense of solitude and the loneliness of the night. I thought about Merrin and Mel and wondered about Ferret and the Dex. I imagined myself blitzing the HSC and actually finding some definition in my life. I thought of Amity and her lovely breasts.

The black water became less threatening and I slipped off my board to feel it around me. It was like floating and sinking at the same time. And I got a tiny feeling inside me, like everything was going to be alright.

Link paddled across and we caught our last waves. We walked home with the pleasure of guilt keeping us quiet. As we crept into the house, I tripped on the weights now set up in the garage. They clattered against the concrete. I froze, my pulse nearly throbbing out of my throat. Link touched me on the shoulder.

'You're okay, Jonah. Just relax.'

I nodded.

He was right.

10

Sam and Link left early on Monday morning. I was glad. It wasn't until I had to face school that I seriously considered the bagging I would cop if people found out about Link. I regretted my text to Amanda, telling her — of all people — that Sam was gay.

Mel met me at the end of our driveway. She handed me my essay, complete with corrections in her round, messy handwriting. And she'd used her trademark orange pencil. I was missing her.

'Thanks for sitting with Mum,' she said as we walked. 'She gets lonely, you know, and it's hard to get away sometimes. I just ...' Her voice trailed and she shook her head. 'Thanks.'

I nodded and kept looking straight ahead. It was one thing to see the pain in Merrin's eyes, but I didn't want to see it in Mel's. Especially if I couldn't do anything about it.

'Link was home on the weekend.'

'I know. Your mum rang my mum. I think she was crying.'

'He's a fag.' I held my breath wondering what would come next, ready for her to make fun of me — the guy with a gay brother.

'A homosexual.' Mel corrected. 'You don't have to use such disgusting language, Feet. He's still your brother.' She launched into a PC lecture that lasted all the way to the bus stop and I couldn't help but smile. Of course Mel wouldn't care that Link was gay. She wouldn't care if he was a one-eyed leper. My smile widened as I listened to her talk about tolerance and respect. It was going to be okay.

Ferret arrived late to roll call. His eyes were no colour, just big black circles as he slid into the seat next to mine.

'Corker of a night,' he whispered. 'Haven't even been home. Started at four yesterday and never stopped. Never stopped, Joe.' His breath was bad and he had ridiculous tufts of bum fluff that should've been shaved or evened out.

'Ferret, you look like crap,' I said, as the announcements were read. 'You've got to get yourself together.'

'I am. I'm like glue I'm so together. Like *g-l-ew*.' He sounded it out as though he was in kindergarten. Then he let his head drop to the desk and shut his eyes. Mel leant back in her chair and asked if he was okay.

'Yep. Reckons he is. He's like glue.'

'He's been sniffing glue, more like it,' Mel said.

'*G-l-ew*, get it right, you peckers.' Ferret didn't even open his eyes.

Ferret chugged off early in the Dato, wagging

period 6. He looked like he was going to be sick. Mel wanted to go with him, insisting someone should check he got home safely.

Dan argued with her, saying she was being stupid and that Ferret had dug his own hole. Mel said that she was being a friend.

'Just remember, Mel,' Dan said. 'Sometimes people are drowning, not waving.'

'That's exactly my point,' she replied, snatching up her bag and marching to the car park.

After school Dan and I surfed off the river mouth at Pambula and then caught the late bus home.

'Do you reckon Ferret's okay?' The bus growled through a gear change and I hoped it covered the concern I could hear in my voice.

'My care factor for Ferret is about negative ten at the moment.' Dan didn't hesitate.

'That good, hey?'

'He's a user, mate. Users are users. He uses the Dex and he uses us.'

'Us?'

'Well, he's using you and Mel.' I'd seen Dan angry before, but I'd never heard him slander a mate like that. This whole thing was blowing out wider than I'd realised.

'Ferret's not using me,' I said.

'Yeah, he is. You just don't know it yet.'

The bus brakes hissed as it stopped and Dan got off in the main street. I could see Stacey waiting for him in a coffee shop. I watched her blow him a kiss and saw how he pretended to catch it.

Dan didn't know shit.

At home, I could hear people talking upstairs in the kitchen. Mel's voice and Merrin's. I started up, taking the stairs two at a time before the sound of Mum crying stopped me.

'I just don't know what I've done. I was a good mum. I read to him. I sang to him. I breastfed him. Oh, God.' Her voice caught and I could hear her sob. 'Do you think I *made* him gay?'

Merrin's voice came next. I could hear a tiny hint of something underneath her words of comfort. A bit of the devil, perhaps? Some humour?

I crept up another step and peeked into the kitchen where I could see them sitting around the dining table. Mum held an enormous glass of wine in one hand and Mel was painting the nails of the other. Merrin sat at the head of the table, lining the nail polish bottles up in order of height. She looked better today. She had a coloured scarf firmly tied around her head. Her face seemed brighter and her eyes were like round beacons, shining out.

'He's just gay. It's not like he's got terminal cancer.' Mel's voice was steady as she smoothed the polish over Mum's nails. Mum looked at Merrin, her face a picture of remorse. 'It was a joke, Andrea.' Mel smiled at Mum and before long they were all laughing. Mum inspected her nails and carefully lifted her glass.

'I guess it could be worse,' Mum said.

'Worse than what?' I stepped up from my hiding place.

'Oh, nothing.' Mum sighed and topped up her wine. I sat next to Mel and she reached for my hand. Without a word, she started painting my nails a creepy shade of hot pink. It felt good to have her touching me.

'What are you doing?' Mum stared at me across the table. 'Jonah?' Panic was rising in her voice.

'What?' I looked at her, without smiling. 'I love the way this looks.'

Mum paled. 'Oh, Jesus,' she said. 'Not you too?'

Mel looked at me, barely containing her laughter.

'No, Mum.' I started to laugh. 'It's okay. I'm not a poof.'

'Homosexual,' they all said. 'Poofter's not PC.'

Dad came home just as Mel was applying top-coat-quick-dry to my little finger. He called up to me from the front door.

'We're in the kitchen,' Mum yelled down. 'Come up here and see what your son's wearing.'

I flapped my hands around in the air, like the girls did when they wanted their nails to dry. Merrin laughed.

'No,' Dad insisted. 'I need to see Jonah. Now.'

I ran downstairs to find Dad still in full formal police gear. He usually went straight to the safe and took off the scary stuff like the spray and the gun.

'Hey, Dad.'

'Look at this.' He shoved a digital camera in my face and showed me the image on screen. It was the big 'police targeting' sign at the top of Merimbula hill. It permanently read *POLICE TARGETING:* and then there was a blank space where the cops would insert little plaques like *SPEEDING* or *DRINK DRIVERS*. But the image on the camera screen wasn't clearly visible.

'What?' I looked at Dad who was glaring down at me.

'Zoom in.'

I pressed the zoom button, admiring my pink nails at the same time. Then the image became clear. Someone had neatly printed in large block letters *POLICE TARGETING: REDUCED BUM CRACKS*. I tried not to laugh as I handed Dad the camera.

'A red Datsun spotted at the scene earlier this morning. I suspect it's the same unregistered red Datsun that's been coming around here lately.'

'Yeah, I know, Dad. What am I meant to do? It's not like I was with him when he did this.'

Dad put his mouth right next to my ear. He pressed his hand on my shoulder and I could feel his police belt right above my own waist.

'You tell him Senior Sergeant Worthy isn't happy. The mates rates are about to stop. No more warnings.'

Dad stepped into his bedroom then, undoing his belt and loosening his shirt. He called something up to Mum and it was only then that my Dad arrived home.

Before that, he'd been the local senior sergeant. And he had given me an official directive.

Mel and Merrin stayed for dinner. Merrin rang Geoff who arrived with five large pizzas. Mum opened three bottles of wine and I couldn't believe it was all happening at my place on a Monday night.

I sat out on the deck with Geoff and Dad for a while. Dad was mellow with wine and repeated the 'as long as he's happy' speech. Geoff replied with his own series of sorrows, contemplating Merrin's future health. It sounded like both of them were trying to convince themselves that things would be alright.

Mel and I left when Mum opened a bottle of scotch and Geoff began singing YMCA. Dad was looking for hats they could wear so that everyone could join in the gay sing-a-long. Surely that wasn't PC.

Mel and I walked down to Spencer Park and sat out on the jetty. The tide was in and the water swelled softly beneath us. There was a half-moon and each ripple of water looked like a tiny snow-capped mountain. A warning light overhead cast a dim blue circle over the jetty. We sat on the edge with our legs dangling over the weathered planks.

We talked for a bit about stupid things: teachers, assignments and the exams. And then we got to the topic of Link.

'I always had such a huge crush on him.' Mel sighed. 'And it was all for nothing.' She laughed. 'There're a few girls who are going to be disappointed when they find out.'

A rhythm of worry pulsed within me. I was dreading the moment when the whole town would learn my brother was a poofter. I'd only just found out. I didn't want everyone else to know. I wasn't ready.

'You're not going to tell anyone, are you? About Link?' I didn't want to sound desperate, but Mel knew me too well.

'Oh for God's sake, Jonah, relax. I won't say anything. It's no big deal. You're as bad as your mother. You think you've got the world on your shoulders.'

'Well it feels like that sometimes.' I was a spoilt brat and I knew it.

'Yeah, I know. Everyone feels like that.'

There was silence for a moment and I wondered if she was going to storm off again. An old dinghy was tied to the jetty and the hull knocked gently against the pylons. It was a steady rhythm, like a heartbeat.

'What's your biggest worry?' Her face was turned away from me but her words carried off the water.

'My biggest worry?'

'Yeah.'

'Right now?'

'They change on the hour?'

I laughed. 'Promise you won't tell?'

She nodded, looked my way.

'I haven't slept with anyone.'

'What?'

'I'm still a virgin. You know what I mean?' My heart was pounding.

'That's your biggest worry?' Her voice was strained. She didn't believe me.

'Yeah, right now it is.' I sounded defensive. You put your whole heart out there and she just eats it up.

'So what about that girl from the sports camp and the girl from the Caravan Park?'

I shrugged and shifted my weight against the old, dry jetty planks. 'Just rumours really. I mean, I tried, but they just …' I didn't know what to say. Silence settled again with the old dinghy still beating away. Mel picked at an old fish hook embedded in the jetty.

'What's yours?' As I asked the question, her fingers kept tugging steadily.

'The what-ifs.'

'Huh?' I kept watching her hand, nails digging into the splinters of wood, prising at the rusty old hook.

'The what-ifs. What if she dies? What if she doesn't? What if she dies while I'm doing the HSC? What if I can't help her? What if I can't be strong enough? What if I stuff it all up? What if I tell her it's going to be alright and it's not?'

The fish hook broke then, snapping off in her fingers with the sharpest part still wedged in the wood. I reached out and took her hand, taking the broken metal from her and dropping it into the water. We sat for a while, holding hands.

'It must be like every person has a quota.' Her voice was gentler now. 'Like I know I'm nearly at my limit. I've just got to sort the big stuff from the little stuff and that's all I can do. You know what I mean?' She looked at me and I nodded, but I didn't really know. I couldn't.

'Mum's cancer is a big thing. The biggest. And then everything else is just like...' She opened her hands and shrugged. 'All small, you know? Like the HSC and uni choices and the formal and going out and all that crap. It's nothing. It's nothing, you know?'

She stared at me again, her eyes angry now, daring me to disagree — challenging me to give her some perspective. She jabbed her finger down onto the broken hook, wedging her nail beneath the tiny stick of metal.

I took her hand and gently pulled her towards me. I wanted to fix everything. But all I could do was kiss her.

I tried to kiss away her sadness. Tried to let the what-ifs become my own, even just for a moment. But she felt too good. And I kissed her more and more, laying her down on the dirty, old jetty and letting my feelings lead my body.

She was soft and warm and beautiful. It was like the night-surfing all over again. The dark and unknown waters somehow becoming familiar. Becoming my home.

'Stop, Joe.' She breathed the words. I felt them melting into my mouth, tasted their meaning before I heard them. I leant back, letting the cool night air make a space between us. 'I can't do this. Not now.' I sat up wondering what was happening. Blood was pounding through my body.

'I'm sorry.' I didn't know what I was apologising for, but she had sounded so sad.

'No, I'm sorry.' She took my hand, lacing her fingers through mine. 'I just can't.' Her voice caught and she sobbed. 'I can only do one big thing right now.' Her breath was shuddery, her voice a whisper. 'And it has to be my mum.'

I nodded, noticing how still the water had become. Glassy. 'Couldn't we just, you know?' I squeezed her hand, not daring to let it go. 'Couldn't I be like one of the little things? Just a little worry? Nothing big?' Even as I said it, I knew I was stretching the limits. Knew that she didn't have room. But her answer surprised me.

'Not for me. You can't be a little thing.' She had stopped crying.

'Okay.' I hauled her to her feet and noticed her kick at the tiny stub of hook. We walked home holding hands. There were a million things I wanted to say but I suddenly felt we had all the time in the world. And no matter what she'd said, something had changed between us.

My driveway was at the bottom of the hill and there were no lights on in either of our houses. Mel let go of my hand and stepped away.

'You want to make a deal?' I asked, reaching again for her hand. She stepped closer to me and I put her arms around my waist.

'Depends?' She smiled up at me and I wondered if she knew I was drowning.

'If we're both still virgins by the time we're twenty-one, will we … you know?'

She laughed then, burrowing her head into my chest as I hugged her to me.

'Oh, Jonah.' She stepped back, looked up into my eyes. 'What makes you think I'm still a virgin?'

'Oh, God,' I said. 'Now you're gonna make *me* cry.'

I watched her leave me and walk up the hill on her own.

I lay in bed but I didn't sleep. I looked at Pam but she didn't seem so shiny anymore. I kept remembering the kiss on the jetty, how soft Mel had felt. Her warmth. I imagined us going further and further. Dreamt that we were naked in the water. My heart thundered with the idea. I couldn't wait to see her again. My friend Mel from up the road. My Mel.

11

Apart from my family, Mel was the one person I had seen most throughout my life. She'd always lived up the road and we'd even been to preschool together. But as I got ready for school that next morning, it was like I was getting ready to see her for the first time.

I thought about her as I ran to Short Point and around to the jetty where we'd been just hours before. At home I drank a protein shake and ate a breakfast from the prescribed list Link had left for me. I showered and shaved, scraping off any patchy stubble, and finished with aftershave. I chose a clean shirt, even though it was only Tuesday and gave it a quick touch up with the iron before putting it on. I was ready half an hour early.

I felt like jumping out of my skin with excitement. It was as though there was big surf and no school. As though my every desire would be fulfilled. I wanted everyone to know that Mel was mine but I held it close inside me too, remembering how soft and warm she'd felt beneath my hands. Her voice and her words.

Her words. It felt like I was cresting a wave as

I remembered them, my stomach actually dropping with the memory. *You can't be a little thing.* I decided to text Amity. I had to let the feeling escape me somehow.

I am on with Mel, I wrote and then pondered what to say next. I was turning into a girl with all this romantic excitement. I pressed send and waited. She wrote back quickly.

Good. Now you can stop hitting on me. LOL. Serious — she is a friend 1st. Friend for eva remember that C U soon x x x.

It was chick-shit and I knew it, but good advice as well. The sort of thing Mel might even say. Friends forever.

Ferret's red Dato came screaming down the street. I watched him toot for Mel and felt my heart swell up as she burst out of her front door. Ferret revved the car hard and accelerated down to my house. I ran around the back of the car, wanting to end up behind Mel who was in the front. I threw my gear in and hastily scrambled after it. I gave her shoulder a squeeze before reaching for my seatbelt.

Ferret was shouting something out the window and I looked out to see Dad, standing on the deck with his cup of tea.

'Is that vehicle registered, Michael?' Dad asked. 'I know you'd hate to lose it.' His warning tone was mixing with the steam from his cuppa.

'No fear, SS Worthy.' Ferret's voice was cocky. 'You know me. I stay on the right side of the law.' He saluted Dad and drove away carefully. Around the corner he accelerated, churning up our neighbour's nature strip as he went. I closed my eyes and sighed, knowing Senior Sergeant Worthy would not be happy.

'Slow down.' Mel's voice was calm. 'I don't feel safe.' I tried to touch her again, but I couldn't do it without Ferret noticing.

'It's okay, babe,' Ferret bragged. 'You're safe with me.' Without giving way, he turned onto Main Street, adjusting the stereo volume as he went.

'Car looks good,' I said, noticing the new CD player and car-seat covers. Large, fluffy dice were hanging from the mirror.

'Yeah, I know.' Ferret smiled at me in the mirror, his eyes crazy and wild. I pretended to admire the plush new seat covers.

'So I guess you got it insured too? Registered?' I tried to sound casual.

'Why?'

'I dunno,' I answered. ''Cause it's illegal not to. 'Cause you could get a fine.'

'Who's gonna tell on me?' His eyes in the mirror again, hardened now. Threatening.

'Just get it registered.' Mel was still calm, the perfect antidote to the flicker of rage that was burning like a pilot light inside me.

Ferret accelerated and made a sharp right, crossing over double lines.

'Ferret, for God's sake,' Mel reached up to grip

the hand hold as he sped up the hill. 'Where are we going?'

'We're picking up Jumper Girl. I'm on with her, you know? You don't mind shoving into the back, Smelly Melly?'

'Jumper Girl?' Mel's full attention was on Ferret.

'Yeah.' Ferret slipped down to first and stormed up the street.

'As in Libby?'

'Yeah.'

The music kept pumping out of the stereo, but no one spoke. Ferret slowed and pulled into a driveway. A cluster of ancient flats stood before us, like crusty old sea barnacles. Rust had formed over the handrails and the white paint was beyond flaking — it was flapping in the breeze.

'Ferret?' Mel grabbed his arm as he stepped out of the car. 'Libby and you? She's … you know?'

Ferret turned the key, killing the music.

'I know. It's okay.' He pulled away from Mel and slammed the door. 'Back in a tick.'

Mel got out of the car, dragging her bag with her. I opened my door and slid along the seat, wondering what it was I'd just observed. I couldn't get my head around it — Mel and Ferret. Had they ever been a couple?

Mel sat next to me and yanked the door closed. For a moment neither of us spoke. I tried to think what Link would do. Or even Dan. I could sense her warmth in the space between us.

'These are nice seat covers.' I let my hand wander through the thick fluffy texture. Mel eyed me with a smile. Feeling encouraged, I pushed my fingers further along until they were almost touching hers.

'What are you doing?' She looked pointedly at my hand.

'Nothing.' I tried to act sly. 'I'm just admiring these new car-seat covers. They're very soft, don't you think?'

Mel let a little laugh escape. 'Mmm,' she murmured as she let her fingers move across the wool. She leant towards me and my heart raced out to meet her. 'They are soft.' She paused, letting her voice become dramatic and whispery. 'They're really, really … soft.' She breathed the word onto me, letting her face fill my vision, before collapsing onto me in fits of laughter. I felt my shoulders slump and gave way to laughter myself.

'A guy tries to be a little suggestive and look what happens.' I grabbed her hand and laced my fingers through hers. She had stopped laughing.

'I've got no room for suggestions, Jonah. Big things, remember?' She tried to pull away.

'Nuh.' I tugged at her hand, pulling it close to me. 'It's me, Mel.'

'What's going on in here?' Ferret's voice boomed into the car and we instinctively drew away from each other. Jumper Girl was getting into the front seat as Ferret turned the ignition and changed CDs. I looked at Mel, but she was staring out the window.

'Hi guys.' Jumper Girl turned around in her seat and smiled at us. As usual, she was wearing the jumper. It was stretched down so long, only a tiny bit of school dress was showing underneath. I mumbled some kind of a greeting while Mel launched into some chick-shit chitchat.

Ferret drove at legal speeds all the way to school. He adjusted the heat and music, each time checking with Jumper Girl to see that she was comfortable. I wondered what could be under her jumper that had the power to turn Ferret into such a gentleman.

The senior students were called to an assembly immediately after rollcall. I was surprised to see Dad there dressed in his senior sergeant outfit. Two other officers stood beside him.

'What's this about?' Dan asked as we filed in.

'Dunno.' I shrugged.

Amanda tugged at Ferret's sleeve and whispered something. Ferret nodded and smiled, passing the whispered message on to Libby.

'Oh, so you know, do you?' Dan's tone was acid as he turned to Ferret. 'Tell us then, what's it all about?'

'Poofter patrol.' Ferret laughed.

Amanda snorted and slapped Ferret's arm. I could feel Mel moving closer towards me.

'Poofter patrol?' Stacey looked at Dan, desperately wanting to be in on the joke.

'What are you on about?' Dan looked at Ferret as

though he'd mutated into some kind of alien.

'All in good time.' Ferret's tone was measured and controlled. 'All in good time.' He sat himself down on the dirty gym floor and pulled Libby in towards him.

I was rigid with fear. I couldn't concentrate on anything. Even the warmth of Mel's body nestled close to mine couldn't melt me. *Ferret knows*, I thought. *Ferret knows Link's gay.*

'Are you listening to this?' Mel tapped Ferret on the back of his head and pointed to the cop who was speaking out the front.

'Yeah.' Ferret flicked her hand away.

'And so ...' It was a female officer talking. She was gesturing out towards the student car park. 'We'd like you all to consider this as your first and only warning. The speed limits are there to be obeyed. Cars must be registered. Must be insured. P-plates should be clearly displayed. We're visiting all the local schools and you can expect a blitz in the coming weeks. We're serious about this. No second chances. Any questions?'

Libby walked next to me as we filed out of the assembly.

'Is that your Dad?' she asked, flicking her head back towards the posse of cops loitering in the assembly hall.

'Yeah,' I said. 'He's the senior sergeant. It's like living in prison.' I smiled as she laughed.

'You don't mean that.' She had a pretty face and

nice hair. I'd never really looked beyond the jumper.

'Nah, it's not that bad. It's just that he's always over your shoulder, if you get my drift. One false move and you're dead.'

'Yeah, I know what that's like.' She looked sad then and I wondered what I'd said wrong this time.

We trudged into our classrooms. Within minutes it seemed that the police presence was forgotten as the weight of study and exams resumed its fearsome grip. I hoped that the 'poofter patrol' joke had died a natural death. But all day long I felt like I was holding my breath, like I was going to be dumped by a wave.

At exactly 3.35 that afternoon the whole thing surfaced again. Dan and I were waiting for the bus home. It was raining and we had gallantly offered to let Ferret take his harem of girls home in the Datsun. Libby and Amanda seemed okay about accepting the ride. Stacey wasn't so sure.

'It's registered, isn't it?' Stacey's eyes were wide, almost reflecting the magnitude of her stupidity.

'It will be, won't it, Ferret?' Mel pushed her out the school doors, somehow parenting both Stacey and Ferret at the same time.

'It's registered for love,' Ferret crooned, skipping ahead of the girls and dancing through the rain across the car park.

Dan and I watched them go and then headed to the front entrance to wait for the buses. We dumped our bags down, claiming a space right next to a life-size statue of St Peter himself. The statue had arms outstretched as though reaching for Jesus across the water. Someone had perched a broad-brimmed, girls' sunhat on the statue's head and I noticed his fingernails had been decorated with permanent marker. A saint dressed in drag? This gay thing was all around me.

'So the story is that Link's a poofter.' Dan kicked his school bag as he said it.

'Nah,' I kicked my own bag. Hard.

'Yeah, that's what I said.' Dan looked at me.

'Who said it anyway?'

'Amanda.'

'Well, it's not true.' I kept my head down, kicked my bag again.

'Ferret's saying it too.'

'It's bullshit.' I put the boot into my bag once more and watched the zipper bust open.

'Yeah, I know.' He nodded.

Behind Dan I could see another image of St Peter, a massive painting. He was standing near a fire outside some kind of courthouse. It was the other big story about St Peter. The time he denied Jesus, his best friend. And not just once either, three times, right before they crucified him.

I looked down at my bag, textbooks spewing out of it. I was just as gutless as St Peter, lying about Link and the person he really wanted to be. But I reminded myself that Link was no Jesus Christ. And it wasn't like he was going to be crucified. Not yet anyway.

Later that night, the guilt returned. Why couldn't I just be proud of Link and who he was, instead of ashamed about something he couldn't change?

School continued to be a gruelling way to pass the time. Everything seemed to be injected with pressure. Assignments that would contribute to final grades, essays that would prepare us for exams, impromptu tests to assess recall and understanding. I felt like they should have been handing out machine guns and grenades. I was starting to think the HSC needed slaughtering. Kill it before it kills us.

With daily phone bullying from Link, I settled into a reasonable routine. Run, school, surf, study. And on alternate days, I'd do some weights. Not that I would admit it to Link, but it really seemed to work. He rang me each night, requesting an update on all my 'stats' including run time, study hours and wave quality. I think he saw himself as a bit of a life coach, so I tried to reassure him that he was just a gay guy and a loser.

I wasn't sure if everyone else had someone like Link breathing down their necks, but as winter settled around us it seemed like the whole world was hibernating. No one was in the mood for partying and even Ferret seemed to have calmed down.

Jumper Girl — Libby — sat with us most days. Or rather, she lay with us. She would find a patch of sun and sprawl out on the ground. Ferret would curl up next to her. They talked together quietly while Ferret rubbed her back or stroked her hair. It annoyed Stacey no end.

'Get a room, you two,' she spat. 'Some of us are trying to study.' She had a textbook balanced on her lap and was copying answers onto the inside of her arm. I looked at Dan, who actually rolled his eyes at me and shrugged. I wondered if there was trouble in paradise.

As far as I was concerned, Jumper Girl was a good distraction. Her presence had taken the pressure off me. No one had mentioned Link or the 'gay brother' thing. All the gossip seemed to centre on Libby and Ferret and why the two of them were together.

Things with Mel were exactly the same. But different. She worked hard to avoid me and I loved it. Her every effort to keep me away was another reminder of that night on the jetty. I was a thing in her life and I knew it. Not a big thing, but something not small enough to be ignored.

We studied together most nights. Mel insisted we work in 'common areas', as though I might just have my wicked way with her if we were left alone in a bedroom. It was probably for the best, because having her near me was a study in itself.

I was meeting her for the first time in so many ways. Noticing the shape of her arms and the way she rubbed her top lip when she considered something difficult. I saw her eyes light up when she worked out a problem and watched her tuck that orange pencil behind her ear, only to search frantically for it a few moments later.

It was just Mel — the way she'd always been. Nothing new really, except for a new thread sewn between us. A strand of possibility.

Dan was hassling me about Amanda Wellings. She kept trying to hang out with us and rang me at least three times a week. She claimed she wanted to apologise for the rumours she started about Link being gay. It was beyond chick-shit though. Every word Amanda spoke was raw sewage.

'Are you on with her or what?' Dan asked one day during lunch break.

'Nuh.' I glanced at Mel who was plaiting Libby's hair. We had started calling her Libby, although Ferret still called her Jumper Girl. He was pathetic with her really, and had a heap of nicknames: Jump Start, JG, Jumper 'n' Bumper.

'I think Amanda really likes you.' Libby turned to look at me. Mel kept plaiting. I shrugged, hoping the conversation would change.

'Nah,' Ferret added, gently touching Libby's plait. 'Joe only does Sirens. Isn't that right? How is she anyway? Been getting much lately?'

At that moment Stacey sniffed loudly and made a little scene as she stood up and stalked away from us. It seemed to be some kind of peaceful protest but like everything with Stacey, we had no idea what it was about. Dan watched her go without saying a word.

'So you're not on with Amanda?' Dan asked again.

'Nuh. I'm not on with Amanda. Hey Mel, want to plait *my* hair?'

Ferret once told me that Sirens can be conjured up from the water and maybe he was right. Just hours after Ferret had been talking about her, Amity turned up.

We were all walking to the student car park, arguing about who was going to bum a ride with Ferret and who would catch the late bus. Of course Ferret and Libby were in, so it was down to Dan, Stacey, Mel and me. Amanda was trailing along with us too, which made things more difficult.

The Dato was still unregistered and I was more than willing to be the designated bus-rider. I had enough to deal with without provoking Senior Sergeant Worthy.

'What if he just takes the girls?' Stacey was saying. 'There's us three girls and you boys could surf or something, before the late bus.'

'Are you stupid?' Dan stopped walking and turned to Stacey. 'It's about minus four in the water these days. We can't surf without a steamer. So, unless you've got a couple in your bag, we won't be surfing jack-didley-squat.'

There was an awkward silence as we hovered

around the Dato. Libby slowly opened the front door as Ferret unlocked the boot. Mel and I were suddenly fascinated by the car duco. Stacey started to cry then and Dan walked away from her. We kept standing in our positions, hoping someone else would say something to fix things up. Of course it was Ferret who came up with the goods.

'I reckon you chicks can have the car,' he said, noticing Amity's sedan pulling into the school driveway. 'Us blokes can go home with the Siren.' He jumped on the bonnet of the Dato and made a loud siren noise, thrusting his hips around as he had done that time in Catholic Studies.

Amity pulled up beside our group and wound down the window. Stacey suddenly stopped crying and flicked her hair around her shoulders. She moved closer to Dan and Amanda did the same.

'Hey, who wants a lift?' Amity stepped out of the car looking less like a Siren and more like poor white trash in her baggy trackies and frumpy footy jumper. I could almost hear Stacey and Amanda breathe a sigh of relief.

'Yeah, I will. And Mel.' I grabbed Mel's hand and let my fingers loop through hers. I had to drag her towards the car. Amity smiled brightly and settled herself behind the wheel.

It was like leaving the scene of a train wreck, with Amanda sticking her tits out and Stacey starting to sniffle again. I looked back at them as we pulled away. Ferret gave a few good thrusts before jumping off the bonnet and Dan gave me the finger. He was smiling though, and I hoped he wasn't too annoyed.

Amity introduced herself to Mel as she drove us home. Mel took it all in, her body relaxing by degrees. It was like watching ice melt and before long she was chatting with Amity and sharing her life story.

'Sorry I haven't been in touch, Jonah.' Amity glanced at me in the rear-vision mirror. 'My mobile got stolen and I lost all my numbers. And then things were crazy with uni and work, so I haven't been able to get away. I wanted to catch up with you, but I didn't want to turn up at your house, so I thought I might find you at school. I don't suppose there's any chance of a surf?' She paused for a breath. 'I've bought a steamer and I'd like to try a different board. I can't believe how addictive surfing is. Have you ever surfed, Mel?'

And they were at it again, comparing notes about sports they'd played and things they liked. They both squealed with delight when they stumbled across their shared passion for reading. I think I said about two words the whole ride home.

We surfed off Short Point while Mel watched from the shore. Amity tried a few different boards and it was clear that the time away from the water had done her good. She approached each wave with determination, knowing it could be a long time between sets.

Dan met up with us out the back. Apparently

the icy waters couldn't keep him away from a Siren in a wetsuit. We talked for a bit and I introduced him again to Amity. She tried Dan's board and failed miserably. Dan took over, giving her pointers on balance and movement.

I paddled away from them, keen to have a play even though the waves were ordinary. The tide wasn't right and each wave seemed more swollen and waterlogged than the last. I rode them in steadily, remembering how it felt to learn.

I'd been on a one-way street back then, going nowhere but forward. Couldn't turn, couldn't carve. Link would shout instructions at me. A stupid grin would infect my face, showing the world how proud I was, even though I wasn't achieving much.

And I surfed straight for a long time. For one entire summer I just went forward. Paddled out and then surfed straight back to shore. I didn't think I could turn. And I was certain I'd fall if I tried.

'You need a road map or something?' Link had asked me. 'Aren't you ever gonna turn? You get more bang for your buck: a longer ride. Just turn, Feet. Turn.'

I had tried to turn and of course I fell. Pummelled in the whitewater like a sock in the washing machine.

'Least ya tried, mate.' Link had scooped me up and paddled away.

Surfing was a prick of a thing to learn, I thought, as I watched Amity clambering back onto her board.

It was elusive. More of a feeling than a skill. A feeling you wanted again and again, but there were no guarantees.

I was still reminiscing about surfing in straight lines when Mel looked up from her book. I waved, bowing before leaping off my board. She laughed and so I caught her eye again on the next wave, this time pulling a face before tumbling into the shallows. Her book was down now and she was grinning at me. I rode four more, each time acting out something ridiculous. I peeled and ate a banana, danced the chicken dance, did the Hokey Pokey and finished with a fine imitation of Ferret and his hip thrusting. Mel was laughing again and it made me laugh too.

We all piled into Amity's car with surfboards wedged between the seats. Dan and Amity were locked in conversation about surfing techniques and the body mechanics of it all. Amity was completely pumped and her questions showed genuine passion.

We all got out at Mel's house, even Amity. Mel lured her in with the promise of a hot shower in a real bathroom.

'You don't want to know what goes on in that amenity block at the Caravan Park,' Mel said. Amity looked puzzled as Dan laughed.

'Hey,' I said. 'Ferret's a good bloke. It's those skylights that are the problem.'

Amity turned white as she realised what we were saying.

'Oh,' she stammered. 'No. He doesn't? Does he ...'

She looked at Dan who nodded. 'Oh, I'm never showering there again.' We were still laughing as we entered Mel's house.

And then there was a tiny moment — just a fraction — when we realised Merrin was dozing in her armchair. I could see Amity and Dan taking in the medicines and the oxy tank and all the other crap that was sustaining her life. I hoped Mel hadn't noticed their hesitation, but she was busy waking her mum gently and adjusting the blankets and quilts around her.

Merrin was sluggish and slurry and I wondered if we should've maybe gone to my place. I suggested it to Mel who immediately shook her head.

'It's okay? Isn't it, Mum?' And Merrin nodded, her beacon eyes still lighting up. God, she looked old.

Mel introduced Amity and directed her to the bathroom. The three of us sat with Merrin for a while, watching game shows on TV and eating Vegemite on toast.

When Amity returned, we studied. Amity said it was her way of paying for the surf lesson. She read over different essays and made suggestions here and there. She helped Dan for ages with a tricky logarithm, even though maths wasn't her strong suit. I think Dan was yanking her chain. I watched him as Amity leant across him to retrieve a pen. Her tits were squashed against his arm and he looked at me and licked his lips, as though Ferret had possessed his body.

Dan left after the fourth phone call from Stacey and I decided to go too. Geoff was now home and cooking dinner, while Merrin continued to doze. Mel and Amity were deep in conversation, something about metaphors and imagery in poetry. I heard Mel telling Amity that she had written a few poems herself and I wondered what else I didn't know about her.

At home, I checked on the hour to see if Amity's car was still in Mel's driveway. At midnight, it was still there and I stopped checking. I went to bed and wondered if it was a good thing to let two worlds collide.

The next day at school, Mel passed me a note. It was a Stacey kind of note, with decorated love hearts and little flowers and squiggles all over it. Only the orange pencil and the little picture of a skinny Beach Rat impaled on a surfboard let me know that it was really from Mel. The note contained just one word. *Okay.* I searched through the flowers and swirls, trying to decipher a further meaning, but there was nothing. I looked at her across the classroom, but she was engrossed in what the teacher was saying.

Okay. It haunted me throughout the lesson. What did it mean? What had I said? Did it mean: okay, she wanted to see me for real? Like a couple?

I chased her down at recess, cornering her before she reached our usual hangout.

'What does it mean?' I waved the scrap of paper impatiently.

'It's like a contract,' she said simply. 'You should keep that somewhere safe. I think you'll need it.'

'What?' I was getting impatient. This woman was wearing me down in ways I didn't know were possible.

'Don't you remember? The deal.'

It flooded back into my mind, like a fast tide. The night on the jetty, that moment in the driveway. Sex by twenty-one.

'And this is a contract?' I didn't know what to say.

'Yep. If you're twenty-one and still, you know … I'm your girl.' She wafted past me, leaving me stranded with endless possibilities.

I was delirious with the prospect Mel had presented, so I didn't register Ferret's manic mood until halfway through the recess break. Libby wasn't with us and Ferret was back to his usual bad behaviour. He spat mandarin seeds at anyone passing by and then sent one directly into Stacey's face. Dan tried to tackle Ferret but he was too quick. Stacey gathered her things and huffed off.

'What's your problem?' Dan asked.

'Nothin'. What's your problem?' Ferret was drumming madly, his hands a blur as he straddled the timber seat.

'I've got no problem, Ferret,' Dan said. 'You're just being an idiot.'

'Oh, so that's it.' He drummed a final rhythm and then turned to Mel. 'Does the opinion poll include you too? Am I an idiot?'

Mel sighed and stood up, addressing the three of us as though she was the principal.

'Right,' she began. 'Enough. What's going on with you lot? You're emotional cowards, I know that, but there's obviously something wrong. Let's start. Ferret?'

'Ah, get stuffed, Mel,' Dan said. 'We don't need a counselling session.'

'Oh, but I think you do.' Mel's tone was condescending.

'Yeah, maybe we do Danny Boy.' Ferret began drumming again. 'Like why the hell you lot went surfing yesterday without me?'

'You're joking,' Dan exploded. 'We went for a surf. Whoop-dee-doo! Geez, you're starting to sound like Stace.' And then he put on a high-pitched whiney voice. 'Why didn't you ring me? Why didn't you invite me? Why didn't you surf with me?'

'So what are you saying? We're not buddies any more? Not mates? We don't tell each other stuff?' Ferret stood up, trying to tower over Dan who still seemed bigger, even though he was sitting down.

'Sit down, peckerhead.' Dan scuffed his foot against the hard cold ground and looked away from Ferret.

'Nah, come on.' Ferret shoved Dan's chest and Dan immediately stood up.

'Fellas, hey.' I looked at them both, toe to toe on our usually peaceful little patch of land. 'Let's go to

150

'Coot.'

It distracted them both and they looked at me curiously.

'Tomorrow,' I said. 'We haven't done it in ages. If we can get a car.'

'We'll take the Dato,' Ferret said. 'Get some ockies and strap the boards on top. It'll be right. Yeah.' You could almost see the cogs turning in his brain.

'There's meant to be a good swell coming.' Dan sat down and contemplated the plan. 'Sounds good.'

We were still nodding and finetuning details when the bell went.

'I don't get you guys,' Mel said as we ambled into the building.

'Nothing to get, Mel.' Ferret threw his arms around Dan and me before trying to scrum us into a headlock. 'Nothing to get.'

12

The problems related to a day trip to Mallacoota only hit me later that night. The Dato still wasn't registered and it was not a vehicle that could support two boards, a boogie and three lads. Wagging school probably wasn't a sensible option either. There were things due at the end of the week and the teachers were watching us like hawks. Then, there were Dan and Ferret who could potentially kill each other before we'd even crossed the Victorian border. And the worst thing: a day without Mel.

I called her that night.

'Hey,' I said. 'How's your mum?'

'Yeah, okay. It was a good day. She's playing Sophie B. and humming along when she's not passed out in the chair. The doctor came today and everything's stable.'

'Sophie B.? Again?' I laughed. Mel's mum had an obsession with this singer from the nineties, Sophie B. Hawkins. She went through phases where she played her CDs endlessly. It drove Mel crazy.

'Yeah, better than Neil Diamond. I'm over him.'

I laughed again. 'Can you cover for us tomorrow?'

'Jonah,' Mel whined. 'I don't want to. I'm no good at lying.'

'Please. Please, please, please. I'd do it for you.' I let myself sound like a little boy, knowing that it made her smile.

'Alright,' she snapped.

'Thanks, Mum.'

She laughed and I tried to imagine surviving the day without her.

'Hey, Mel?'

'What now?' Her tone was playful.

'Maybe I could come up to your house tonight? You know, for a little midnight visit?' I let the question hang between us.

'Why?'

'You know why, Mel. I want you.' I tried to say it in a way that sounded sexy, but it just came out desperate.

'No, Jonah.'

'Come on.' I was close to begging. 'I'd surf so much better if I could just do this. I need you.' My dick was halfway up just thinking about her.

'You'd surf a lot better if you weren't so selfish.' She sounded so much like my mother that my dick didn't just go limp, it shrunk about an inch.

'Mel —'

'No.' She cut me off. 'If I'm your girlfriend, then I'm your girlfriend. That doesn't mean I owe you anything.'

And suddenly I didn't care about the sex. I was

just stoked that she'd called herself my girlfriend.

After Mel, I rang Link. I thought he might preach at me and talk me out of the trip to 'Coot, but he was pretty cool.

'Yeah, it should be good there this time of year,' he said. 'What boards are you taking?'

When I explained that we only had the Dato and were limited to one board each, he got a little serious.

'Just be careful, hey, Feet. You don't want the old man finding out. Is the Dato registered yet?'

'Nuh.'

'Ferret driving?'

'Yeah.'

'Well, just be careful.'

'Righto.'

'And have fun.'

'Yep.' I forced myself to show interest in his life, asking about Sam and modelling. Then it was just a matter of grunting a response in between Link's lengthy explanations. I wondered if there was a male equivalent to chick-shit. Maybe it was called prick-shit. I didn't know if it could affect all blokes, or just the gay ones.

The next day, I headed out at my usual run time taking my board with me and hoping Mum wouldn't notice. I trudged up the hill to Ferret's where icy winds welcomed me in an offshore that was as promising as it was ominous. Dan and Ferret were already there, arguing as they struggled with ockie straps.

'You're such an un-co,' Dan was saying. 'You've got to actually hold it. That's why it keeps coming off.'

'What? I've got to drive the whole way there with my arm out the window like this, keeping the frigging ockie strap on? Dude, if that's the case we may as well ride our skateboards down there.'

'Mornin' lads.'

They looked at me as if I was a life raft and I wondered again how the day would pan out. We strapped the boards on and wedged Ferret's boogie board into the car. Ferret ran through the rendezvous times before Dan and I headed back home.

By 8.30 we were off, scoffing down Maccas and talking up the surf. The road was boring; scrub on both sides with endless tourist drives meandering off in all directions. Painfully slow tourists towing caravans put the handbrake on Ferret's driving.

'I want to pass, but I don't want to get airborne,' Ferret said, thumping impatiently against the steering wheel. We were all a little nervous about the boards, knocking away on the lid of the car. At one stage, when Ferret crept up to one hundred, the boards had thumped so loudly that we actually pulled over to check on them.

'What'd Stacey say about you wagging today?' I turned to Dan in the back seat. He was sprawled out but looked uncomfortable with the boogie board resting against his legs.

'Didn't tell her,' he said. 'The last thing I need is her in my ear.' He changed the pitch of his voice to mimic Stacey's. 'Why didn't you take me? Where did you go? Why couldn't I come?' He impersonated her well and he knew it too.

We travelled on in a comfortable silence. The kilometres threaded behind us and the thought of the ocean pulled us forward.

'Oh, yes!' Ferret exclaimed suddenly, shifting vigorously in his seat. 'Wood on the road.'

'Oh, you freak,' said Dan from the back. 'Do you have to tell us about it? I don't want to know what's happening in your pants.'

'It's a freebie,' Ferret said. 'No stimulation needed — they're the best sort. Give it a suck why don't you, Jonah?'

My elbow jabbed straight out and stabbed him in the chest. Ferret doubled over and coughed, trying to catch his breath. I leant across and gently steered the wheel.

'Well that got rid of it,' he said eventually. Dan started laughing and Ferret joined him. After a while, I laughed too.

'Libby's angry with me,' Ferret announced. 'And it's all because of you, Joe.'

'Me?'

'Yeah. Why'd you have to bring the Siren into school? She was fully up me for the rent because of your hot chickie babe.'

'Geez, I'm sorry.' I looked at Ferret whose face was totally serious. 'But, do you reckon maybe next time you ought to save your thrusting and siren call for somewhere a little more private than the bonnet of your car? Libby might not have liked that.'

'You reckon?' Ferret grinned at me.

'So what's up her jumper anyway?' Dan asked, from his lounge on the back seat.

'A baby,' Ferret said.

'Don't crap on,' Dan drawled. 'What's up there? Big scars? Huge tits? No tits?'

'Nah, for real,' Ferret said, glancing back at Dan. 'She's pregnant. Nearly due. Her folks sent her down here from Sydney when they found out. They're heavy duty Catholics.'

'No way,' I said, trying to bring him back to reality. 'She's not fat enough.'

'Yeah. She's up the duff alright. She just hides it really good. She's got to go back to Sydney after it's born. They're going to adopt it out. You should see the bump. Freaky stuff. But God she's gorgeous.' He groaned.

I tried to get my head around Ferret's news. I remembered Mel's cryptic conversation the day we first picked Libby up. She must've known.

'Oh, stop the car,' said Dan, sitting up straight and winding down the window. 'I'm going to be sick. Are you for real? You're on with a preggo girl?'

'I prefer to think of her as a Yummy Mummy.' Ferret tooted the horn, just to emphasise the point. 'It's the way to go guys,' Ferret insisted. 'No obligations.'

I remembered my conversation with Libby about the senior sergeant. God, Dad was nothing like her olds. He wouldn't kick his own kid out of home. I felt sorry for her. She needed protecting, needed a friend. And instead, she had Ferret.

That's when the pilot light ignited inside me. Maybe I'd spent too much time with Mel or I'd caught a touch of gayness from Link, but everything Ferret said was wrong. No obligations. It was beyond PC. Ferret was nothing but a mongrel.

Surfing at 'Coot was not for the faint-hearted. The beach we went to was more exposed than anywhere in Merimbula and the waves were more powerful. There were rocks and rips in random places and even boats had a hard time getting out across the bar.

We suited up and unstrapped the boards, all the while keeping one eye on the water. Even Dan took a moment to survey the place before catching a nearby rip and paddling out to the left. Ferret went in next, walking backwards with his flippers on. He'd left his snorkel mask behind, but still had goggles perched on his forehead. He yelped as the water reached his hips and shouted out that it was freezing.

'Wanker,' I said, waving from the shore. I sat for a moment on the winter wet sand and watched them negotiate their first waves. The sets were messy, crumbling and rusted off around the lip, but they were huge. Big canyons, lurching up out of the ocean. Dan was sticking down low, riding well into the throat and steering clear of the lip that was both fragile and explosive. Ferret was still fumbling around with his goggles, sitting up on his boogie board with the stealth and balance of a cat. He finally took a ride, pulling off a three-sixty before catching the same rip out that Dan had bummed in on.

I followed him in, letting the rip run me out with minimal effort. But I headed to the right, letting the rip form a barrier between them and me. I was closer to the rocks and the waves were more treacherous, but I didn't care.

A gorgeous set billowed up and I rode the first one carefully, remembering my basic technique. I channelled out through the rip again, ignoring Ferret who was beckoning me to his side. I let the next few take me, exploring their size and power with small turns and a few re-entries. I let the wave hold me, grounding me firmly into the ocean.

I could see Dan ripping and carving as I paddled back out. He looked good, with the grey clouds bundled overhead and the dark water churning behind him. He was full of aggro and the waves were copping the punishment.

Ferret was the first to leave the water, stumbling out backwards and waving at us, signalling time out. Dan and I stayed in. I attempted a few moves I'd seen the pros do, failing dismally each time. I didn't seem to have the balance or the speed to pull them off.

'At least you tried, mate,' I said to myself, reverting back to more familiar manoeuvres. Dan paddled across to me and we talked about different ways of gaining air.

'It's hard though. You've got to be quick, eh? And balanced.'

I nodded. 'I can't get the speed and the balance at the same time. It's like one or the other. There must be something else to it.'

'Yeah,' Dan agreed. 'I reckon. Oh, what's this loser doing now?' I followed his gaze across the beach. Ferret was dry and dressed, talking to two other blokes at the Datsun. His briefcase was open on the bonnet and one of the other guys was opening a backpack.

Dan shook his head and swore. 'He's dealing now.'

I watched, shielding my eyes from the dull winter glare.

'Come on.' Dan caught a wave and let it take him right to shore. I followed, realising my body was numb from the hours on ice.

Ferret saw us approaching and quickly finished up with the guys. They drove away in an ancient VW, black smoke chugging angrily out of the exhaust.

'How'd you go lads?' Ferret asked, throwing his briefcase into the boot. 'It was good out there, wasn't it?'

'How'd you go?' Dan asked, stripping down to his jocks and throwing his near-frozen wet suit onto

Ferret.

'Yeah, I caught a few good ones. It was just so cold. My nuts were freezing. I could nearly snap 'em off by the time I got out.'

'You gotta have balls to lose them,' Dan said, rubbing a tiny towel over himself. 'I've heard Dex shrinks your balls right off. I reckon it's true, hey, Ferret?'

Ferret slumped into the car, pulling his cap down over his eyes. He stayed there, texting on his mobile while Dan and I got dressed and packed the Dato. Dan sat in the front for the drive home. I sat in the back with the boogie and tried to catch some zeds. The music was blaring and no one spoke.

Ferret dropped Dan off first and we stood around for a moment, organising our cover stories. Ferret dropped me off next, slowing down as he drove the last few metres.

'Hey, Joe, could you do us a favour?'

'What?'

'Could you just take the briefcase in with you? Just for the night?'

I looked at him and tried to think of the moment he'd gone from being my mate to this dickhead that he now was.

'Well, can ya?' he insisted. 'One night. That's it.'

I shook my head. 'Nuh.' I didn't even bother with an apology.

Ferret swore and I could see his eyes growing dark beneath his cap. 'You can't count on mates anymore, that's for sure,' he said, revving the car.

'Nuh,' I agreed, hopping out of the car. 'You can't count on 'em.' Bastard.

'I s'pose fags just look out for one another.' He looked straight at me as he said it.

'You'd know.'

'Yeah, I would, your brother's a good root.'

I wanted to lunge at him, to rip his puny body from the car and throw him down. But he drove off, speeding up the hill with my board still hammering away at the top. I stood in the middle of the road and gave him the finger.

I was dreading school the next day. I didn't want to see Ferret and I considered wagging again. Mel had sent me a text the night before and was expecting to see me, so I made myself go.

'How was yesterday?' she asked as we walked to the bus.

'Crap.'

'Oh no.' She sounded genuinely disappointed. 'No waves?'

'No, the waves were good. Pretty rough, but big.'

'So what's the problem?'

'I dunno.'

She looked like she might have being going to say more, but she didn't and I was grateful. She even let me kiss her while we waited for the bus. A few stray Year 7s were nearby, but we were the only Year 12 freaks without our own ride.

'I want you, Mel,' I said, pulling her against me in the corner of the bus shelter. My dick was nearly busting out of my jocks. I pressed her onto it, hoping she could feel what she was doing to me.

'Jonah, don't be gross.' She pulled away from me and made a space between us.

For the first time ever, I was grateful that Stacey was a part of our group. She bounced over to us at recess, waving envelopes in our direction.

'I'm having a party,' she explained, carefully delivering the invites as though we were back in primary school. 'No gatecrashers, okay? Just us. And a few of my girlfriends. And some of their friends. This Saturday.'

She sat on Dan's lap and delivered his invitation with a kiss.

'I missed you yesterday,' she said in a sooky voice.

'And I missed you too.' Dan rubbed his nose against hers and I had to look away. Mel rolled her eyes and winked at me.

'So what kind of a party is it?' Ferret had been quiet all morning. I think he could sense I was ready to kill him.

'Just a party.' Stacey shrugged. 'And like I said, no gatecrashers.'

'How about a rainbow party?' Ferret suggested.

'What's a rainbow party?' Stacey asked, the

picture of innocence.

'Oh, you'd love it Stace,' Ferret said. 'It's where all the chicks bring a different lipstick and they get busy on the guys. Each fella leaves with a little rainbow in his jocks.'

Stacey squealed as Mel turned to confront Ferret, but he was well out of it today. His eyes were slippery black disks and his hands were a blur of drumming and itching.

'What's wrong, Stace?' he persisted. 'I hear you suck a good cock.'

'Yeah, I do,' Stacey stood and faced him. 'It's a shame yours isn't a good one.'

I felt like giving her a round of applause, but she was already marching away from us.

By lunchtime, Ferret had completely lost the plot. I didn't know what he'd taken, but he was out of control. He shouted out to Amanda across the yard, asking if she wanted a quickie behind the dunnies. Libby was away and Mel did her best to calm him down.

'Just leave it, Mel. He's a lost cause,' Dan was opening his lunch as though nothing was happening.

Ferret was sprawled out on the timber bench.

'Move over,' I said, kicking at his feet.

'What's that faggot? You want some of this?'

I was all over him before I could think. I heard his head hit the ground as I squeezed my hand against his throat. I jammed my knee into his groin and belted him hard in the ribs.

Dan pulled me off him while Mel watched, looking horrified.

'What's going on with you lot?' she yelled. 'What's the matter with you?' She looked at me.

'We broke up,' Ferret said, sitting up and pouting like some thirteen-year-old girl. 'Didn't we, Jonah?'

I threw myself on him, kicking and hitting and hoping I could kill him. Dan dragged me away again but I didn't want to stop. Even with Ferret's nose oozing blood and his eye already swelling, he didn't look miserable enough.

I spat on him and walked away.

13

'Jesus, Jonah. What was it all about?' That afternoon Mel and I walked up to Short. I needed a quick hit and badly. Of course there had been a coronial inquest into the whole thing. Time in the principal's office, behaviour reports and phone calls to Mum and Dad.

Fortunately, the inquest didn't stretch to the home front. Mum started to lecture me the moment I walked in the door, but when Dad came home he stopped her.

'Let it go.' His tone was abrupt. 'Feet knows what he's done. Let it go.' I didn't know if Senior Sergeant Worthy was pissed off or pleased.

'So,' Mel insisted as I trudged along. 'Tell me.'

'It's nothing. You don't need to worry about it.'

We picked our way down the rocks and onto the sand.

'I am worried though.' She zipped me into my steamer. 'You're my friends and I don't like fighting.'

'Ferret's not our friend.' I told her. 'He's a wanker.'

'No, he's not.' She stepped around in front of me.

'He just needs help. He needs his friends.'

'No, he doesn't.' I shook my head. 'Ferret's not worth it. Trust me. He's a little thing, a very little thing. Life's not meant to be this difficult, Mel.'

'Maybe not for you. Life's not difficult if you're ignorant, if you just watch it instead of living it.' She was firing up now. I could see it in her eyes. 'You're just going out with the tide, Jonah. You don't care. You're caught in a rip and you don't even know it.'

'You can't rescue everyone, Mel.'

'I can try.'

I surfed, even though I probably should've sat on the shore with her. I thought she might leave the moment I went out back, but she stuck around. I could see her digging little burrows into the sand and burying her feet one at a time.

I took each wave mindlessly, wanting the past few days to rinse out of me. I let Mother Nature do her work as I bonded with each wave. Only Mel's words kept rolling back in. *You're caught in a rip and you don't even know it.* Maybe I was. Maybe we all were.

Maybe life was just a series of rips. The HSC, a gay brother, a sick mum. They were things that tried to drag us out into dangerous depths. Things we couldn't control. You couldn't swim against a rip.

After an hour, my fingers were wrinkled and I couldn't feel my dick, so I caught a wave in and hoped Mel had calmed down.

'I thought about what you said,' I told her, as we sat together on my board.

'Mmm.'

'You know, about being out to sea? Being stuck in a rip?'

She nodded.

'A rip doesn't last forever, Mel. You just gotta wait till it empties out. Then it's all about swimming to shore.'

'Yeah,' she said. 'I know.'

She was crying.

We headed up the hill together, threading our way over the rocks like we'd done so many times before. Mel waited for me while I rinsed my board. Barefoot, we continued up the headland, pausing occasionally so Mel could pick a bindi out from her foot. At the Caravan Park, she stopped and turned, motioning me to follow.

'Nah, Mel,' I said, surprised. 'I'm not in the mood for Ferret right now. I'm not going to apologise either. He can go and —'

She stopped me with a kiss. It was like another movie moment but it was really happening and it felt sensational. I could feel her body pressing against me. She shivered and my dick exhausted itself in an effort to rise against the thickness of a wetsuit.

'Let's go to Amity's van,' Mel whispered. 'I know where she hides a key.'

I tried not to run as I led her through the Park. She giggled when I fumbled at the lock and we both laughed as we wrestled my surfboard into the van. But then, things turned serious.

Mel was lying on the bed, looking up at me with eyes I'd never seen before. I wanted to take command of the situation, to ravage her like a porn star and hear her begging for more. It was tricky though, with my surfboard propped against the bed and the sound of little kids playing nearby. The moment I'd been hoping for had finally arrived and all I could do was look at my feet. They seemed to be mocking me, the only part of my body not smothered by wetsuit.

And suddenly I was shit-scared. What was I meant to do? And why was I wearing a wetsuit? A full-on bloody steamer. I was covered — neck to ankle. Only a leopard seal would think I was sexy.

I'd had plenty of wild and crazy dreams about what sex would be like. And in my mind I'd undressed women a hundred times, but never in my kinkiest fantasies had I ever imagined I'd be dressed in a wetsuit.

How the hell was I meant to get naked? There's no sexy way to strip off a wetsuit. Not in a caravan. In fact, there wasn't even enough room for me to undress safely.

And then another horror image — my dick would be damp and shrivelled from the surf. Pubes would be clinging to it. I'd heard girls say that dicks could look gross, and I knew mine wouldn't win any beauty contests. It'd probably look like a small animal with mange. Even Link wouldn't have a quick remedy for a half-up hard-on covered in a web of pubes.

I didn't even have a condom. Where was Ferret with his twelve-piece handout when you needed him? What did Mel expect me to do, make a franger from my wetsuit? I could feel my dick shrinking.

She wriggled towards me and tugged at my hand, turned me around and undid the suit. The zip was big and chunky, making its usual loud farting noise as she dragged the tab down. She pulled the suit from my shoulders and my whole body was shoved around. It wasn't the kind of foreplay I'd imagined.

I tried to step out of it with some kind of dignity, but I lost my footing and ended up falling onto the bed. The suit was still dangling from my feet, like a shadow that wouldn't go away, when Mel lay down exactly on top of me.

She was full on, kissing me hard and grinding her hips against me. It was like Amanda Wellings had possessed her body. I felt weird and wondered if this was normal, but my dick was starting to show signs of life, so I let Mel do her thing.

'Are you sure about this?' I asked as she pulled her top off.

She nodded, but her eyes looked vacant. She jumped off the bed and started pulling down her trousers.

'Come on,' she said, lying next to me. 'Do it.'

And that's when I knew it wasn't for real. It wasn't right.

'Mel.'

'Come on, Jonah,' she insisted. 'Let's just do it.' I heard her voice catch and she wouldn't look me in the eye. Something switched off inside me and I knew we weren't going to have sex.

'Please, Joe?'

The best chick in the world was asking me for sex and I wasn't going to do it. It was worse than the dream about the industrial hose. I was living through a nightmare. My dick had already started retreating and I wondered if I'd ever see it again or if it might need therapy for post-traumatic stress or something.

'Mel, hey,' I pulled her towards me and arranged us both under the covers. She felt soft and smooth, like the ocean on a calm day.

'I just want to feel something.' Her voice was small, barely a sound. 'Something else, you know? I just want to feel something else.'

'Instead of what?'

'Instead of dread.'

We held each other for a long time and then we walked home. In the dark, together.

14

The Friday before Stacey's party, Ms Finlay asked our Catholic Studies class to stay back late.

'It's completely optional,' she said. 'If you can take a late bus or if you drove, it'd be great if you could stay behind.' She gave us time to organise ourselves as people contacted their folks and made alternative arrangements.

'Okay,' she announced when everyone was ready, 'let's go to the beach.'

It was a short walk from St Peter's to Pambula Beach. We dumped our bags in the Surf Club and headed down to the water.

'Alright,' Ms Finlay was shouting against the wintry breeze that was whipping in off the water. 'You've got six more weeks at school. Ten weeks until exams. Fourteen weeks until school's finished.' Someone let out a cheer and the group laughed.

'So,' she gestured to the ocean and the sand dunes. 'Life will go on. This'll all still be here. No matter what comes your way, the ocean still keeps rolling. You can't change that. No amount of worry and stress will ever change that.'

The group was silent, each person considering her words.

'You don't have room for worry and stress and panic and anxiety, guys. You just don't have room. Because life just keeps coming.' As though listening to her every word, the ocean slammed a mighty wave against the rocks. Some of the spray drifted over us. Ms Finlay laughed. 'And if you're carrying all that around with you, you're never going to get anywhere.'

She instructed us all to find a stick and a patch of sand. We were to write down everything that was bothering us, everything that was holding us back from really living the life we wanted.

'And remember, start small and close to the water. Work your way up to the dunes. Think of the little stuff. Get it down first and watch how quickly the ocean eats it up. Now get started: this tide's coming in.'

I wandered off with Mel to find a stick.

'You and Finlay are on the same page,' I said. 'Now you can send the what-ifs out to sea.'

'It's not that easy you know.' Mel snapped off a stick and headed down the beach.

At 5.00 most of the group had gathered back together.

'So,' Ms Finlay said. 'What did you notice?'

'My biggest problem's still there,' one kid cried. 'I put the little stuff down first and the big stuff's in the dry sand. It's like it's bogged there.' A few people laughed, but Finlay nodded.

'And that's how you work out what the big stuff is. You don't worry about the small stuff. That comes and goes. The big stuff's what you give your attention to.'

She dismissed us and sent us on our way, waiting in the parking lot until the last few were collected. Then she came and sat beside me on the old wooden fence. We could see Mel, way down the beach still writing and writing, her body curled over and pondering the sand like a miner fossicking for gold.

'You want me to go to her?' Ms Finlay asked.

'Nah,' I said. 'Just tell me what to say to her.'

'Don't say anything,' Ms Finlay advised.

It took half an hour to get down to Mel. She was beside the outfall pipe by the time I got to her. It was nearly dark. Her worries had started a good kilometre down the beach and she was still writing when I got to her.

'Hey,' I spoke lightly, touched her shoulder. 'You were meant to write them this way.' I indicated with my arm, showing her how she should have listed them vertically, starting down on the wet sand and working up to the dry. 'You've done them all along the dry sand. The tide's not going to make it up here.'

'I know.' She looked at me and we were back in Year 6 all over again. Her little eyes looking at me helplessly. 'She's dying, Joe. I know it.'

'Come on.' I took her hand and walked with her,

wrenching the stick from her grip and tossing it out to the sea. We passed sandcastles, standing like little headstones, obscure markers of a fun day on the beach. A flock of seagulls hurried home, momentarily suspended as they found themselves caught on a jag of wind. The tide continued grooving its way in, moulding and shaping the sand until we were walking over our classmate's writing, watching their worries seep out to sea. Darkness gathered round us.

'Look,' I led Mel closer to the club house, where I had written my own list. I ran to the club and made the sensor light flick on before standing beside her and pointing in the sand. 'There's my number one thing,' I said.

We both looked down at the letters, carved in the soft sand.

Mel.

Link and Sam were home for the weekend. I took the lead on Saturday morning and raced them all the way to Pambula Beach. We even ran home along the sand, treating ourselves to breakfast at a café in town. Amanda Wellings served us and I'm sure she winked at Sam.

'Hi, Jonah,' she chirped. 'I just saw Ferret. The cops took his car, did you know that? It was unregistered.'

I mumbled hello and opened the menu, letting all three fold-outs shield me. I wasn't in the mood for Amanda and it annoyed me that she was chick-shitting about Ferret. He hadn't had his car taken at all. The cops had just paid him a visit. He'd been texting me all night, wanting me to ask Dad what his legal rights were. He was a dickhead, that was for sure, playing it like we were still mates. I didn't know about that.

'Hi there.' Link stretched out his hand and introduced himself to Amanda. I lowered the menu and watched Amanda try to flirt with my brother. She flicked her hair and let her eyelashes work overtime.

'And this is my partner, Sam.' Link gestured across the table to Sam who smiled up at Amanda. At first she looked astonished, amazed by what Link had just admitted. But then she nodded slightly, with her eyebrows raised as though everything made perfect sense to her. A smug little Beach Rat.

Amanda tried to give me a sympathetic stare across the table but I just looked her in the eyes and told her I wanted a big feed of greasy eggs and bacon. Sam and Link ordered the same.

I scoffed down my food, laughing as Sam described Link's latest modelling stuff-up. And then it hit me. Everyone would know now that Link really was gay. Amanda would make sure of it. I paused for a moment, letting the crispy bacon go cold on my plate. But then Sam delivered his punchline and Link rolled his eyes with embarrassment and I just wanted to laugh at what they were saying. I was sick of trying to take it all so seriously.

Back home, Link let me skip the weights, but insisted I study while he went down the street. I didn't even argue. Study was just something that had to be done. The HSC was going to happen whether I liked it or not. I'd almost stopped worrying about it. It hadn't been very high up on the list of things I'd written in the sand.

'I'll be checking what you've done,' Link said, closing me into my bedroom. 'And no jerkin' off either.' He nodded at Pamela who was still beaming down at me. He farted loudly and pulled the door shut, holding it tight so I couldn't escape.

After dinner, we headed up to Mel's. Link and Sam wandered arm in arm and I was thankful it was dark so I didn't have to watch them.

Merrin was in her usual spot, her armchair now replaced by a special chair-bed from the hospital. Her face had almost withered away, her skin tight and brittle. I thought of a skeleton and immediately felt guilty. All kinds of bags and tubes were attached to her. She barely opened her eyes when we arrived, but she gripped my hand tightly when I leant down to kiss her.

Mel looked beautiful as she stepped into the room dressed for Stacey's party.

'I won't be too late, Mum.' She kissed Merrin and arranged her blankets, almost casting the glow of life over her. I looked away. Life and death, face-to-face.

Mel and I walked to Stacey's. I hummed a Neil

Diamond tune just to be annoying. But Mel looked happy and light and I wondered if the sand writing might have been a good thing after all.

The party was in full swing. Ferret had already been ejected and Dan was wasted beyond belief.

'We've had a fight,' Stacey told us, gesturing to Dan as she took us through to the kitchen. 'Hey!' Her panda eyes, blackened with soggy mascara, lit up. 'Did you hear about Libby? She had a baby. A baby boy! I didn't even know she was pregnant. Do you think it's Ferret's?'

Mel pressed her drink to her lips and shrugged.

'And something else.' Stacey grabbed my arm, drawing me away from the others. 'Amanda's been going around saying stuff about Link. But I don't believe it, okay?'

I wanted to tell her that I didn't care, but Mel had me by the hand and was leading me out of the kitchen. Dan was slumped on the lounge, nursing a beer.

'So is it true?' Dan asked, managing to look at me without raising his head from his chest.

'What?'

'About Link, being a poofter?'

'Yeah. He's gay.' I waited for the nuclear fallout, not sure if I was ready to take Dan on. I wondered briefly what gay-bashing really meant; it seemed that I was the one doing all the fighting and I wasn't even gay.

Dan nodded down at his beer and shrugged. 'At

178

least he's getting a bit,' he mumbled. 'Man's not a camel.' He looked miserable.

'What's the problem, Dan?' Mel turned to face him, ready to listen.

'Stacey,' he replied. 'I give up. I'm never going to get laid. I've already wasted four years.'

Mel threw her head back and laughed while I tried to understand everything that was happening. Dan and Stacey weren't having sex. For all I knew he was still a virgin.

'It's not funny,' Dan slurred. 'I'll be a hundred before I get anything. Hey, Mel, you want to make a deal?'

I sucked at my beer and smiled while Mel and Dan negotiated.

People came and went around us. Dan shuffled off, promising to bring back a beer. Music played and couples danced. The faint smell of pot wafted through the room. The lounge was ours and I pulled Mel towards me.

Just when I thought my balls would burst, she drew away.

'Joe, we have to stop.' Mel looked around, pushing me back.

'Where's Dan anyway?' I asked, shifting my body and noticing the rest of the room that existed beyond Mel. 'What's he doing? Brewing the beer himself? Like he said, a man's not a camel.'

'You get drinks,' she instructed. 'I'm going to the loo. Meet you back here.'

In the kitchen, Amanda Wellings was dry humping something that was wedged uncomfortably on a stool.

'Hi, Jonah,' she said, drawing enough breath to reveal Dan's happy face squashed beneath her. She went back to work and I cracked open my beer.

I flopped back on the lounge and waited for Mel. My phone sounded, barely loud enough above the music. It was a text from Link. Just five words.

Bring her home. Bad news.

'Sorry I took so long.' Mel's energy filled the room. 'Stacey was in the bathroom bawling her eyes out, something about Dan and Amanda.' She looked at me shyly and reached for my hand. 'Do you want to go?'

And I put that moment in my mind as a memory I'd keep forever. The moment before Mel's life changed. The moment when I thought, maybe just for a few seconds, she was truly happy.

I showed her the text message and watched her face. She looked straight at me and I saw her terror. I wanted to reach inside and take the most fragile part of her and hold it. To keep it safe so it wouldn't get broken.

We walked without speaking, retracing our steps back home. She took my hand as we turned into our street. Ambulance lights flashed over us.

'Are you okay?'

'Yeah.' She took a shuddery breath. 'A rip doesn't last forever.'

15

Mel didn't cry.

She didn't cry when she walked into the lounge room and saw her Mum's chair was empty. She didn't cry at the funeral either. Not when they played Sophie B. Hawkins. Not even when she helped to carry out the coffin.

Everyone kept saying we were celebrating Merrin's life but the whole thing felt hollow. Like we were watching a movie without the main character, just a big space where Merrin should have been.

I thought about my life: surfing and exams and sex. I thought about the big stuff too — how a mother could die, that my brother was gay, about Mel and my dickhead mate who was into the drugs.

And even though it was a funeral and everything was up to shit, I had a feeling that things might be alright. I was alive and there was a future ahead of me. I could survive, I'd get there. Get somewhere. Like that moment when you catch a wave. You don't know where you'll end up, you just enjoy the ride.

The week before the HSC began, I dragged Mel

outside for a study break. We were huddled in between our rocks at Short Point, with the ocean screaming and raging below us. She had been on autopilot ever since Merrin died and I was certain that a part of Mel had passed away as well.

'Do you have a plan, Joe?' She was staring out to sea.

'A plan?'

'You know, for next year.'

'Nuh,' I shrugged.

'Me either.' She smiled sadly. 'The plan is, there is no plan.' She tried to laugh, but the sound was hard, almost angry.

'But that's alright, Mel. You don't have to have a plan. You'll be okay.'

'Really?' She looked at me hopefully and I hugged her to me, trying to take away her sadness.

'Why don't you cry?' I asked, kissing her face. 'You'll feel better.'

'Because,' she said, 'if I start, I'll never stop.'

I kissed her face again, letting our lips eventually meet and feeling my body slide into equal measures of pleasure and frustration.

'Joe,' Mel whispered.

'Yeah, I know,' I said, drawing away and blatantly rubbing at my crotch. 'We have to stop.'

'No,' she said, 'I don't want to stop.'

It was different this time. We still laughed as we snuck into Amity's van, but the mood was intense. Mel moved slowly, completely unaware of how gorgeous she was, of how she was turning me on. She took off my clothes and even though there was a weird moment when I was down to my jocks, things were so much better than the other time — with the wetsuit.

She put her hand on my heart and then kissed my chest.

'You taste like the ocean,' she told me.

'Are you sure about this, Mel?' It was obvious that I wanted her and I didn't know if my dick could wait for her reply.

She was softer than I had imagined and the feeling was all consuming. I was submerging myself into a whole new ocean and it was the closest I'd come to drowning. I was lost inside her. When I finally made it back to shore, I knew that something about myself would never be the same.

We laughed our way through the awkward moments afterward. Mel seemed to have her wits about her, while I was still recovering. I wondered what it had been like for her and immediately wished I could've lasted longer. Wished I had thought more about her. On a scale of one to ten, my performance probably ranked less than ordinary. I watched her as she moved and spoke, drawing me back from oblivion and into reality. She was still my Mel, but she was something else as well. An ocean I had never known.

We settled down beneath the sheet, our heads resting on the same pillow.

'Thank you, Jonah.' She smiled at me, her hair tufting out at crazy angles.

'Well, I did my best.' I grinned at her and she laughed. 'How do you feel now?' I shifted my head back, wanting to see her whole face.

'Okay,' she said. 'Alive. Like I might be able to feel things again, feel happy again.'

'You will.'

'Yeah, I know. One day.'

She reached for my hand beneath the sheet and it was the closest I'd ever felt to anybody. I couldn't explain it. It might've been love.

Link and I surfed that next morning. He and Sam were down for the weekend. We got up early, just as daylight approached. The waves were unseasonably round and hollow. I surfed them with reverence, letting memories collide with the future.

'Remember when you only surfed straight?' Link asked, thieving into my thoughts.

'Yeah.' I smiled. 'Remember when you *were* straight?' I splashed him and made a grab for his leg rope.

'You little shit.' He reached for my leash and tugged.

A pristine set wandered out from the depths and we both paddled hard, still grabbing each other's ropes. I tried to escape him, but we were riding the same wave.